"I'm your baby's fat[her]," [Theo said] quietly.

Those four words made Emmie catch her breath. Was she wrong to deny Theo even the chance to try to raise their son in the same home, just because she was scared?

But—what about her baby?

Maybe Theo could never love her. But what if there was hope for him as a father?

Could Emmie really deny their baby the chance to be raised in a secure home with both parents? Could she actually be selfish enough to put her own needs first?

"Just go through with the ceremony," Theo told the minister arrogantly. "We'll fix the paperwork later."

"I'm not sure—" the man began, then looked at Theo and shrugged. He turned to Emmie, his eyes grave behind his spectacles as he placed his finger on the correct page. "What do you say, my dear? Should I begin again?"

Lump in her throat, Emmie stared at him uncertainly.

"Do it," Theo said in a low, husky voice. "Say yes. Marry me."

Also by Jennie Lucas

Harlequin Presents

Christmas Baby for the Greek
Her Boss's One-Night Baby
Claiming the Virgin's Baby
Penniless and Secretly Pregnant
The Italian's Doorstep Surprise

Conveniently Wed!

Chosen as the Sheikh's Royal Bride

One Night With Consequences

Claiming His Nine-Month Consequence

Secret Heirs and Scandalous Brides

The Secret the Italian Claims
The Heir the Prince Secures
The Baby the Billionaire Demands

Nine-Month Notice

JENNIE LUCAS

HARLEQUIN

PRESENTS

HARLEQUIN®
PRESENTS™

Recycling programs
for this product may
not exist in your area.

ISBN-13: 978-1-335-59364-1

Nine-Month Notice

Copyright © 2024 by Jennie Lucas

For questions and comments about the quality of this book,
please contact us at CustomerService@Harlequin.com.

TM and ® are trademarks of Harlequin Enterprises ULC.

Harlequin Enterprises ULC
22 Adelaide St. West, 41st Floor
Toronto, Ontario M5H 4E3, Canada
www.Harlequin.com

Printed in Lithuania

MIX
Paper | Supporting
responsible forestry
FSC® C021394

Nine-Month Notice

CHAPTER ONE

EMMALINE SWENSON HAD always known her place in the world. With four rambunctious younger brothers, a struggling father and overwhelmed mother, Emmie's job was to help her family, not herself.

She'd always known she wasn't pretty, with limp dishwater-blond hair and a shape inclined to plumpness from her time baking in their tiny kitchen. As a teenager, she'd dreamed about falling in love with a strong, honorable man and sharing a passionate first kiss in the moonlight. But even then, she'd known romance was unlikely for a plain, dutiful girl like her.

Then, at twenty-seven, she'd fallen in love. She'd been seduced beyond her dreams. For one perfect night, she'd felt desirable, beautiful and valuable—cherished in the arms of the most dazzlingly gorgeous man in the world.

By the next morning, it was over.

Now, at twenty-eight, any romantic daydreams Emmie had ever had were well and truly gone.

"Are you ready, sweetheart?"

Turning away from the mirror, Emmie saw her father at the door, his craggy face beaming with pride and love.

"I wish your mother could see you now," he whispered, wiping his eyes. "She'd be so proud."

"Thanks, Dad." A lump rose in Emmie's throat. She wasn't sure her mother would, in fact, be proud of her today. While she'd lived, Margie Swenson had always tried to convince Emmie to look beyond the grind of endless work and household tasks and find the quiet beauty of life.

Emmie hoped to follow her mother's advice someday. Just not today.

Her wedding day.

Looking at her, the happiness in her father's eyes faded. "Is something wrong?"

"Of course not." Forcing a smile, Emmie rose from the vanity table and stepped into a pool of bright June sunlight from the changing room's window, which shimmered gold against her white satin skirt. It had been her mother's wedding dress decades before and was a little too tight for Emmie in her current condition. She should have had it tailored to fit her expanding waistline, but it had fit her fine just two weeks ago, when she'd agreed to marry Harold Eklund.

A man she didn't love. A man she'd never even kissed.

Emmie's knees shook as she picked up her small bouquet of beautiful red roses sent as a wedding gift from her best friend's grandfather, who ran the flower shop in their vibrant Queens neighborhood. She risked another glance at the full-length mirror. The faded gown was lumpy and unflattering on her pregnant body, making her belly and breasts seem huge beneath the straining fabric.

Her face looked scared and pale in the mirror, in spite of the makeup she'd carefully applied following a video tutorial. The dark eyeliner, mascara and red lipstick made her look strange. Her dark blond hair was pulled back severely beneath her mother's veil, the tulle headpiece perched awkwardly on her head, like a wad of tissues sticking in all directions.

She bitterly regretted not taking Honora up on that offer to hire a professional hair and makeup stylist. Too late for that now. Emmie's best friend should have been her matron of honor today, but she'd rushed to the Caribbean last night with her family to check on Honora's grandfather, who'd been injured on a cruise with his new wife in Aruba.

"Granddad's doing better," Honora had told her anxiously last night. "But I'm so sorry to miss your wedding."

"Please tell him thanks for the flowers, and I hope he gets well soon."

"I promise we'll celebrate as soon as I'm back." Her best friend had paused. "Are you sure about this? Seems awfully sudden."

Emmie had lied and said she was sure, but the truth was she wasn't sure at all.

So maybe it was good Honora wasn't here. Emmie was having a hard enough time pretending she was a happy bride. She couldn't even quite convince her father, though he wanted to believe it with his whole heart. There was no way she could have fooled Honora.

But she'd rather marry someone she didn't love than shame her already grief-stricken family. For the last month, Emmie Swenson had been the scandal of her *neighborhood*, since the warming weather made her burgeoning belly impossible to hide. When her father and brothers demanded to know the name of the man who'd "seduced and abandoned" her, Emmie said she'd had a one-night stand in Rio while she was there working on a real-estate deal with her boss, Theo Katrakis. Which was true, as far as it went.

Theo.

She didn't want to think about him.

Holding her rose bouquet with one hand, she gripped her father's arm with the other so she had the strength to walk. Her breathing came in quick, shallow gasps as Karl Swenson led her out into the church foyer.

"Careful, sweetheart." He flinched as her fingers dug into his arm. He added apologetically, "I'm not as bullet-proof as I used to be, now I'm off the whiskey."

"Sorry." Loosening her grip, she forced herself to smile till her cheeks hurt. "You know I'm proud of you, Dad."

He patted her hand, his blue eyes watery. "I'm proud of you, too. He's a good man. You can build a good life together."

Emmie hoped so. Her mother's death seven months ago had caused enough grief and pain for her family. Since Emmie had revealed her pregnancy last month, her brothers had gotten into multiple bar fights defending her honor, while their shamed father had nearly started drinking again.

She was grateful to Harold Eklund for giving her a way out. The elderly widower, a friend of their family, had been living on his own for years. His apartment was filthy, his clothes rarely clean, and he survived on cola and cheap sandwiches from the bodega across the street. He'd offered Emmie a home, in exchange for her tending house and cooking his dinners. There was no question of love, and certainly not of sex.

But Harold was a kind man. Missing his own faraway grandchildren, he'd offered to help out a bit with her baby. They could help each other. She'd be able to work from home, doing her father's bookkeeping, for at least her baby's first months, long enough for her to figure out what to do. She wouldn't stay married to Harold forever—or would she?

Since their engagement was announced two weeks ago,

her brothers no longer came home at night bloodied and scowling. Her father could again hold his head up high.

Surely that was something she could be proud of. As long as her family was happy, Emmie could live without love.

And good riddance. Love had only broken her heart.

"You sure about this, sweetheart?" Her father looked at her as they stood in front of the chapel doors. "Harold is a good man." He hesitated. "But marriage lasts a long time…"

Taking a deep breath, she nodded. "I'm sure."

Biting his lip, Karl Swenson nodded with an uncertain smile. Turning in his rumpled suit, he opened the chapel doors.

The triumphant organ music crashed around them like a wave. As Emmie entered on her father's arm, the people packed into the crowded pews rose noisily to their feet. Swensons and Eklunds had lived in their little Queens neighborhood for a hundred years, and everyone had come to see the disgraced, pregnant Swenson girl marry the long-widowed, much-pitied retiree.

It was funny. When Emmie was a little girl, she'd sometimes longed to be *seen*. But now, as everyone openly gawked at her from baby bump to badly fitting wedding dress, she wished she could hide under a rock. Some people whispered slyly behind their hands, others smiled encouragement. Being the center of attention was both exhilarating and terrifying.

Theo made you feel like that, a small voice whispered inside her. *The night he…*

Emmie pushed the memory away. She couldn't think of Theo, not now, not when she was about to marry another man.

She looked up at Harold Eklund, waiting for her at the

end of the aisle beside the minister. He was beaming at her, shifting his feet, his thin gray hair combed back carefully, his suit dated and tight.

As she moved slowly down the aisle, Emmie glanced down at the engagement ring on her left hand, with its tiny diamond. "Betty would want you to have it," he'd told her two weeks ago, rheumy eyes wet with tears. "No good gathering dust, she'd say. She'd be grateful to you, taking me on, just until I can see her again."

With a deep breath, Emmie forced her leaden feet onward. As they reached the front of the church, the organ music abruptly stopped, and suddenly it was deathly quiet.

The minister blinked down at her, then intoned, "Dearly beloved, we are gathered here today…"

Emmie barely heard the words. She was dimly aware of her father passing her hand to Harold's care. He held her hand awkwardly, gingerly.

Marriage lasts a long time.

Emmie's heart was pounding. She tried to remember why she was doing this, binding her life forever to a man she barely knew—

Because as she looked up at her groom, she didn't see Harold's pale blue gaze but someone else's, dangerous and black. She trembled, remembering the darkness. The heat—

"If anyone can show just cause why this couple may not be lawfully joined," the minster intoned, "speak now or forever—"

"Stop. Now."

The low growl of a man's deep voice caused the stone floor to shake beneath her feet. Sucking in her breath, Emmie turned.

A powerful man stood at the back of the church, clothed

in darkness, those same fierce black eyes she'd remembered now piercing her soul.

Theo.

He'd come for her!

Theo Katrakis knew the morning he woke up in bed with Emmie Swenson in Rio that he'd made a big mistake.

But so what? His life was strewn with mistakes. He shrugged them off and moved on. Mistakes hadn't prevented him from becoming successful. Indeed, Theo often thought they made him *more* so.

Everyone talked about the necessity of a balanced life, filled with some work, yes, but also friends and family, small pleasures and hobbies, taking care of one's neighbors, and love—love to last a lifetime, love most of all.

But that was no way to build a billion-dollar fortune. The way to do *that* was exactly the opposite: to ignore everything else and focus obsessively on one thing every single day for sixteen or eighteen or twenty hours, then snatch up some sleep. Then wake up and do it again. And again and again.

Friends were not necessary, nor small pleasures, nor hobbies. He'd never met any neighbors in his Manhattan highrise. His other grand properties around the world were all comfortingly isolated by thick walls and security guards. As an orphan, he luckily had no family to worry about. And love, love to last a lifetime?

That was the least desirable thing of all.

There was a reason Theo had reached the age of thirtynine without a wife or child. He had better things to do. He'd been an orphan living rough on the streets of Athens when, at sixteen, his father's brother brought him to live in Upstate New York. After his uncle died, Theo had thrown himself into building his small property-development company, taking it national by the time Theo was twenty-five and global by thirty.

Work was what mattered. Work brought power and money, and those made a man bulletproof.

So when Emmie had quit without notice, calling from New York after her mother's funeral, just days after their night together, Theo told himself he'd survive. It was a damned inconvenience to be sure, but he'd find another new secretary and move on.

And he had. He'd moved so fast and so far he hadn't been back to New York City in the last seven months. It wasn't that he was avoiding her. That would be ridiculous. It had just happened that for the last seven months, he'd been unusually busy making deals overseas.

Then his friend Nico had called him yesterday.

And Theo suddenly realized that the mistake he'd made sleeping with his secretary seven months before was even bigger than he'd ever imagined. One that would permanently change his life.

He'd been on his yacht when he'd gotten the call, en route to the pleasurable endeavor of destroying his new property on the small island of Lyra. Then, as the red sun set over the dark sapphire Aegean, he'd learned his former secretary was getting married. Because she was pregnant.

His friend Nico had snorted. "You didn't know? You really have been out of touch. She told Honora she had a one-night stand in Rio. I guess she hooked up with a stranger at a bar and never learned his name."

Emmie, pregnant from a one-night stand in Rio. Theo felt his body flash hot, then cold. "Impossible."

"I can barely believe it myself. Emmie's always seemed so quiet and sensible." He paused. "It must have happened right before her mother died. Her last days working for you. I don't suppose you ever saw a man hanging around her?"

"No." Theo remembered the tremble of her lips when he'd embraced her, the awkwardness of her movements, her uncertainty. She hadn't known what to do. She'd been a virgin, at her age. She hadn't even known how to kiss.

Then the morning after their night together, she'd gotten the awful call about her mother's death. There was no way Theo could believe, after she rushed back to New York for the funeral, surrounded by her grieving family, she'd suddenly flung herself into the arms of some other man. No.

The baby had to be Theo's.

And she'd never told him.

"She's marrying some old man in Queens," Nico said. "Some friend of her father's. Even Honora can't understand why. We offered to help, but she won't take charity. I thought maybe you could offer Emmie her old job back, just in case she's marrying under financial duress."

Marrying under duress.

"I have to marry him, baby. We won't survive if I don't."

Theo heard the echo of his mother's trembling voice. He leaned against the railing of his yacht, gripping his phone in his hand. Pushing the memory away, he said, "It's a free country."

"What happened between you two?" Nico said suddenly. "I thought Emmie quit to take care of her family. But it seems strange she didn't invite you to the wedding."

"We were never good friends," he said evasively. "You know that."

"But still, it seems like... Oh, no." Nico sucked in his breath. "You seduced her, didn't you? Tell me you didn't seduce her."

Damn him for seeing too much. He gritted his teeth.

"Theo?"

"No," he said heavily. "I didn't seduce her."

And he hadn't—not exactly. But what had happened that night was still entirely his fault. His alone.

Theo had long since come to terms with who he was. Three years ago, his last real girlfriend had thrown a plate at his head when he'd dumped her at Le Bernardin on their six-month anniversary.

"You're a selfish, heartless bastard, Theo Katrakis!" she'd screamed in her French accent.

The plate had missed, smashing against the wall, but the words hit their target.

How could he deny words that were so obviously true?

Being a selfish, heartless bastard had made him who he was today. If women chose to love him after he specifically warned them not to, well, that was *their* mistake.

Then his previous secretary had stormed off the job in the middle of a critical deal in Tokyo, all because she claimed to have fallen in love with him. He'd lost millions in his most expensive love affair ever, which was ironic since he'd never even slept with the woman.

Searching for a replacement, he'd been dutifully attending Nico's summer party in the Hamptons when he'd suddenly looked at Emmie Swenson, the plain, prickly friend of Nico's wife, and realized she had three excellent qualifications: she was utterly trustworthy, she was a whiz with numbers, and she despised him to the core.

It had made him laugh how annoyed Emmie had been to accept his job offer. But she'd needed money to pay medical bills for her mother, who'd been sick with cancer, and her father's plumbing business was in trouble. He'd offered to quadruple her salary, so she had no choice.

"Just promise me you'll never fall in love with me," he'd said.

Her violet eyes had turned merry, making her almost pretty.

"That's a promise that's easy to make. Pigs would fly before I'd ever love you, Theo Katrakis."

And they'd shaken hands on the deal.

He'd turned out to be right. Theo's risky bet on her paid off, as his riskiest bets usually did. After a rough beginning, Emmie had learned the intricacies of the new job and became the best secretary he'd ever had: precise, accurate, a champion at protecting him from things he didn't want to deal with. For over a year, she'd organized his schedule perfectly, taken excellent notes and correspondence, and excelled at fierce gatekeeping.

Until that night he'd discovered that beneath the unattractive oversize suits she wore like armor, Emmie Swenson was a soft and sensual woman, unutterably beautiful, with a kiss like fire.

Until that night in Rio—

No. He couldn't think about it.

Gripping his phone, Theo had stood at the lonely railing of his yacht and stared at the red sunset.

Maybe Emmie getting married was for the best, he'd tried to convince himself. Even if her groom was some old man who was just a friend of the family. Maybe the guy could make her happy. Maybe he could share his feelings. Maybe he actually *had* feelings.

Unlike Theo. And at his age, facing down forty, he would never change. At least not for the better.

He opened his mouth to tell Nico he was out of it, that he'd have his new secretary send some bland gift, that he didn't care.

Then—

His baby.

"So you'll call Emmie?" Nico persisted. "Offer her job back?"

"I'll do more than that," he'd replied grimly. "I'll go to her wedding. And talk to her myself."

After finishing the call, Theo told his crew to return to Athens as quickly as possible. Gloating over the ruin on Lyra Island would have to wait. He told his secretary to make sure his private jet was fueled and ready when he arrived.

Flying across the Atlantic last night, he'd barely slept. He took a shower, changed his clothes, paced. The flight took longer than it ever had. He tried to stay calm, but his heart was pounding so hard he could barely catch his breath. From rage.

Emmie had kept her baby a secret.

She'd lied to him with her silence.

She hadn't even given him a chance.

His plane landed outside New York where his motorcycle waited, a mode of travel quicker than any car. He stomped on the gas and sped to Queens, twisting dangerously through traffic, engine roaring in his determination to reach the church in time.

Cold. Cold. He had to be cold. To lose his temper would show weakness; it would show he cared. He would be ice.

He finally reached the old stone church in Queens, crammed between colorful shops and walk-up apartments. He'd been to this neighborhood. Nico's wife had grown up here, alongside Emmie. The neighborhood was blue-collar, working-class, and a happier, livelier place than Midtown Manhattan. As Theo parked his motorcycle, a dog rushed down the sidewalk, barking happily in pursuit of two children on toy scooters.

Grimly, he set down his helmet over his Ducati. Crossing the street, he strode up the church steps and silently pushed open the door.

The minister was already speaking as he entered the crowded church. His motorcycle boots echoed softly against the flagstones, faltering when he got his first look at the elderly bridegroom. What the…? That was the man Emmie had chosen? Over *him*?

The bride turned her face, and he saw his secretary's snub nose and heart-shaped face beneath an appallingly unfashionable knot of tulle sticking out in every direction. She looked uncomfortable, even miserable, and no wonder. Conventional wisdom said that every bride was beautiful, but the white gown seemed lumpy in all the wrong places. It emphasized her huge breasts. *Her huge belly*.

She was giving herself away, along with her baby. Some other man would be the child's stepfather. She'd hidden the baby from Theo in an attempt to cut him out of the equation, to make him powerless—

"Stop," he ground out, stepping into the aisle. "Now."

Everyone in the pews gasped, turning toward him. The minister stared slack-jawed, and beneath her crown of white tulle Emmie turned, eyes wide with horror.

"Theo," she breathed. "What—what are you doing here?"

"Emmie." His eyes dropped to her belly, then lifted dangerously. "Are you pregnant with my baby?"

CHAPTER TWO

EMMIE SWAYED, her heart racing as she gripped her red-rose bouquet. She looked past crowded pews at the Greek billionaire standing in the aisle. The same man she'd dreamed about every night for the last seven months, in hot sensual memories that left her gasping with need.

"Are you pregnant with my baby?"

No! she wanted to shout. *You can't be his father. Because you'll never know how to love him.*

For months, Emmie had kept quiet about her pregnancy, hoping she could dodge this bullet. She'd never lied about paternity—not exactly. She'd just hoped that somehow Theo would never find out. She'd told herself that even if he knew, he wouldn't care. She would just save him the trouble of rejecting her and the baby.

Emmie had to be hard-eyed and sensible. She'd worked herself through community college, taking night classes in accounting. She'd worked for years in a windowless basement for a corporation downtown before becoming secretary for a ruthless, amoral tycoon she despised. In her constantly struggling family, *someone* had to focus on the bottom line.

But even Emmie hadn't been able to be practical in this case. She knew Theo would have given her child support, for legal reasons if nothing else. But though she'd picked up the phone a few times, she just couldn't do it. Even with her father's plumbing business losing money every month. She couldn't call Theo, groveling and begging for cash. Her pride wouldn't let her.

Or maybe she'd just been afraid of giving him that much power over her. Because unlike when she'd quit her job as his secretary, knowing he'd only break her heart further if she stayed—once he knew, she'd never be able to quit being the mother of his child.

But now he was here. Mouth dry, Emmie choked out, "Who told you?"

"Not you. That's the point." Theo Katrakis's voice, slightly accented from his childhood in Greece, was low and angry as he came forward, his hard gaze pinning Emmie by the altar. "You lied to me."

As he stalked past the crowded pews, whispers went through the church like wildfire.

"Her boss!"

"The billionaire!"

And, doubtfully, "*He* slept with *her*?"

His worn black motorcycle boots echoed in the sudden breathless silence. He stopped a few feet away, beneath the steps to the altar.

Suddenly, he was in front of her, close enough to touch.

"I didn't…lie," she choked out.

Theo's black eyes flickered to her baby bump as his low voice cut her to pieces. "You lied."

Shame went through her because she knew he was right, followed by anger because she'd had good reasons.

"So?" she cried, tossing her head in a wave of tulle. "We both know you're not up for it. You don't do commitment or love. What could you possibly offer our child but money?" She lifted her chin. "No, thanks. We're fine without you."

His lips parted with an intake of breath. Almost as if she'd wounded him. No, impossible. He had no heart to wound, though he'd hurt her so badly.

Then his eyes narrowed.

"So you cut me out." His voice was as cold, smooth and dark as the surface of an arctic sea. "You took your judgment of me as license to steal my baby away."

Emmie caught her breath. *Steal?* Was that what she'd done?

"*You're* the father of Emmie's baby?" Harold blurted out beside her. She'd forgotten he was there. Her erstwhile bridegroom seemed to shrink into his tux, goggling at Theo's imposing frame.

And no wonder. Emmie looked up at her former boss.

It seemed a great injustice of the universe that after seven months apart Theo was more handsome than ever. His muscular chest and shoulders were wrapped in a form-fitting black T-shirt, and black denim caressed his powerful thighs down to short black leather boots. His square jaw was unshaven, leaving a dark shadow from hard cheekbones to his sensual lips. Black eyebrows slashed over his harsh, dark gaze.

She felt a sense of despair, of rage and grief that he could still dazzle her and make her want him. She gripped her bouquet, wishing she could smash him over the head with it. She felt a small burst of pain in her thumb as a single thorn pricked her. Putting her thumb to her lips, she sucked the aching spot.

Theo's gaze fell to her mouth. His jaw tightened. He turned to her elderly bridegroom.

"You are no longer required here."

"I can see that," Harold replied with dignity. "You should take over." Patting Emmie's hand, he said quietly, "I wish you all the luck in the world, my dear, in your marriage."

She stared at him, flummoxed. "You've got it all wrong. He's not going to marry me——"

But Harold turned away from the altar to sit in the front pew. His elderly neighbor, Luly Olsen, wearing a flowery dress and pink hat decorated with cloisonné pins of dogs, caressed his shoulder consolingly.

Emmie couldn't blame him for not wanting to face down Theo. Harold was an old-fashioned man and of course assumed Theo would wish to marry the mother of his unborn child.

But her father and brothers were not so trusting.

"Like hell he won't!" From the other side of the pews, her father rose to his feet, his weathered face dumbfounded. "Katrakis. You're the lover in Rio?"

"Her boss!" Beside him, the four big Swenson brothers, well-fed as linebackers, rose of one accord, fists clenched and lower lips stuck out.

Scowling, five Swenson men came forward with the hostility of an opposing football team or army battalion.

"You seduced my daughter. Abandoned her," Karl Swenson accused.

She heard the low mutter across the church. There'd been sympathy for the Swenson family since Margie Swenson died, Margie of the kind word and buttery *fika* pastries. Margie who'd often snuck treats to children and dogs, offering free meals and gentle encouragement to anyone who needed a helping hand.

"There are more important things than money, Emmie," her mother tried to tell her.

But even before she'd gotten sick, Margie had always

been dreamy-eyed. At twelve, Emmie had taken charge of balancing her checking account and paying the bills so the power wouldn't get turned off. By fifteen, she managed accounts receivable for her father's plumbing business. Her father was excellent at getting customers to pay what was owed but not so good at keeping track of it.

Everyone in their Queens neighborhood knew not to mess with Karl or his four sons. Broad-shouldered and quick-tempered, her four younger brothers, spanning in age from nineteen to twenty-six, were protective of their only sister.

Theo didn't seem worried. Arrogant in his own physical strength, he only looked at Emmie.

"Tell me," he said quietly. "I want to hear you say it."

She looked up at Theo's darkly beautiful face, his penetrating black eyes and the sharp lines of his cheekbones and shadowed jawline. His aquiline nose was slightly crooked between the eyes, broken in some long-ago fight and never set quite right. Her gaze fell to his cruelly sensual lips that she could still feel against her skin, kissing and caressing every inch of her virgin body.

The light from stained-glass windows left a whirl of red and purple and blue against her white satin skirts. Emmie closed her eyes.

"Yes," she whispered. "He's yours."

"He?" Theo had a sharp intake of breath. "A boy?"

"Yes," Emmie's father growled. "And you're going to give my grandson a name and marry my daughter *right now.*"

Emmie's eyes flew open in horror. "No, Dad—"

"Or else."

"Or else," her brothers chorused behind him, clenching their hands.

Emmie flung a terrified glance at Theo, knowing he'd respond with a sarcastic insult that would make her father lose his mind. Any moment, the blows would fly, and someone she loved would be hurt. She spread her arms, trying to create a wall between him and her family. "Please, I promise you, Theo, I don't even *want* to marry—"

Theo gently pushed her aside. Tilting his head, he gave Karl Swenson a hard nod. "Deal."

"You'll marry her?" her father responded suspiciously.

Theo held out his hand. "Agreed."

Her father brightened. "Well, then."

The two men shook hands, as if they'd just agreed to the sale of a used plumber's torch at cut-rate prices or maybe a truck-mounted sewer jetter with barely a touch of rust.

Looking between the two men, Emmie's forehead creased. "Is this some kind of joke?"

Theo glanced pointedly at the minister, the guests, the church, and lifted his eyebrow as he inquired sardonically, "Do I look like I'm joking?"

Whispers and gasps sizzled through the crowd. By now, many wedding guests were holding up cell phones, because otherwise how would anyone believe it, that a plain, twenty-eight-year-old spinster like their Emmie had managed to entice a handsome Greek billionaire into bed—and into marriage?

Reaching out, Theo took her hand. Slowly, he pulled Harold's engagement ring off her finger. She trembled feeling his fingers slide down her hand. Then he turned back to the elderly man.

"Thank you for standing in," he said gravely, giving him the ring. "I'll take it from here." Holding Emmie's hand, Theo turned to the minister. "Go ahead."

Go ahead?

Emmie tried to pull back her hand. "Are you crazy?" she hissed. "I'm not suddenly going to switch grooms!"

"Why?" he asked coolly, as if *she* were the one being unreasonable.

Emmie didn't know why he seemed as if he wanted to marry her, but after a year and a half as his secretary, she knew Theo Katrakis always got what he wanted, when he wanted it.

But not this time. Oh, no. Not this time.

Yanking her hand away, Emmie said, "We don't have a license. Or a ring! And, oh, yeah—we don't love each other!"

Theo's dark eyes slanted sharply to Harold in the front row with Luly Olsen in her big pink hat. He lifted an eyebrow skeptically. The meaning was clear.

Emmie stiffened. Marrying Harold without love was entirely different—she knew the man could never break her heart! Desperately, she turned. "Dad."

But her father only patted her shoulder. "You'll thank me later, sweetheart. It's for the best."

"For the best," her younger brothers repeated, nodding sagely.

She was being railroaded. Looking around the church, she saw no allies. Everyone clearly believed she'd been about to settle for a marriage of convenience with Harold, and so they expected her to clap her hands with joy at a chance to marry Theo instead.

How would anyone understand that it was far worse for her to marry Theo Katrakis, even if he was the father of her baby, even if he was handsome, even if he was a billionaire?

With a deep breath, she whirled back to him.

"Please don't do this. You'd regret it," she choked out.

Black mascara smeared her fingertips as she wiped her eyes. "You'd make me regret it."

He looked down at her.

"I'm your baby's father," he said quietly.

Those four words made Emmie catch her breath. Was she wrong to deny Theo even the chance to try to raise their son in the same home, just because she was scared?

Scared if she ever let herself get close to Theo again he'd wrap her heart around his little finger and never let go. And if he made her love him again, there'd be no escape for her this time, not if they were married with a child. She'd be chained to him forever, by the bonds of matrimony and family and by her own heartsick longing.

She'd spend the rest of her life loving a man who could never love her in return. The endless rejection would destroy her, until it finally crushed her into pieces so small she really would be invisible.

But—what about her baby?

Maybe Theo could never love her. But what if there was hope for him as a father?

Could Emmie really deny their baby the chance to be raised in a secure home with both parents? Could she actually be selfish enough to put her own needs first?

"Just go through the ceremony," Theo told the minister arrogantly. "We'll fix the paperwork later."

"I'm not sure…" the man began, then looked at Theo and shrugged. He turned to Emmie, his eyes grave behind his spectacles as he placed his finger on the correct page. "What do you say, my dear? Should I begin again?"

Lump in her throat, Emmie stared at him uncertainly.

"Do it," Theo said in a low, husky voice. "Say *yes*. Marry me."

She turned, seeing all the staring eyes in the pews, feeling like she was in some awful dream. "I don't know—"

Her voice cut off as he roughly pulled her into his arms. She gasped, breathing in the scent of leather and engines and woodsy aftershave and something even more intoxicating. Something just *him*. Theo's black eyes blazed.

Then, lowering his head, he kissed her.

Theo deployed his kiss like a weapon.

He'd meant to use his sensuality against her, to assert the power of his will and make her agree. He'd done it a few times in the past with other women for much less reason, lazily, almost without thinking. He could always convince a woman to see things his way. And now that he'd decided to marry Emmie, in shocked determination to permanently secure and protect the son he'd just found out about. He had no compunction about his method, just the outcome. The end justified the means.

But as his lips touched hers, something happened that Theo hadn't expected.

The contact of their kiss caused a flash of electricity to curl through him, sizzling up his nerves, burning through his body. It had happened that way before, that night he'd taken her virginity, when they'd conceived their child. But he'd almost convinced himself in the months since then that he'd deceived himself, that he'd been drunk, that he'd been crazy, that he'd imagined that overwhelming ecstasy.

But he hadn't imagined anything.

Kissing Emmie Swenson had made his world spin.

With an intake of breath, Theo pulled her tighter, feeling the firm curve of her pregnant belly and lush fullness of her breasts against his chest, the white satin of her wedding gown sliding against his T-shirt. He gripped her body against his as if she were the answer to the question he'd been asking all his life.

He needed this. Needed *her.* Oh, God. He heard a soft moan and realized it had come from his own throat.

Shocked, Theo wrenched away.

Applause and catcalls rolled through the pews as Emmie looked up at him. Her blue-violet eyes were luminous beneath the ridiculous pile of white fluff on her head. He saw the same agony, the same need and fear, reflected in her beautiful, haunted face. She bit her lower lip, her red lipstick scarlet as roses, emphasizing bow-shaped lips in a heart-shaped face as she searched his gaze. She swallowed, then backed away.

"No," she breathed.

Throwing her bouquet on the floor in an explosion of red petals, Emmie turned and ran from the altar, leaving everything and everyone behind as she disappeared through the side door.

Theo's jaw dropped.

"Guess she needs a little convincing," her father ventured, in what seemed like the understatement of the year. Theo scowled.

Damn it, why was it always so difficult to convince Emmie of anything? To be his secretary? To tell him about her pregnancy? To marry him?

She'd resisted becoming his wife just as she'd once resisted becoming his secretary. Back then, he'd thought it was proof of her good sense, that she saw through his charm and wasn't easily fooled.

But now…

It seemed Emmie's opinion of him hadn't changed at all. Even after their year and a half of working together, she still thought he was not only a selfish bastard but an utter villain. How else to explain why, after their kiss, she'd looked at him with trepidation almost like fear?

Standing abandoned at the altar beside the minister, as the people in the pews gleefully held up their phones, Theo felt foolish, as he hadn't in decades. His cheeks burned.

He'd never imagined asking any woman to marry him, but he'd always assumed that if for some reason he deigned to select a lucky bride, she'd immediately and gratefully jump into his arms.

Instead, Emmie had *run away.*

"Excuse me," Theo told everyone grimly and turned to pursue his fleeing bride out the side door.

He caught up with her on the other side, in the church hall decorated for a wedding reception.

"Wait," he growled.

Emmie looked back at him, her face troubled. "I'm not going to marry you."

He caught her hand. "Just stop."

"Don't touch me." She wrenched her hand away, her brilliant eyes flashing in the dappled light. Such an intoxicating shade. He thought dazedly of violet flowers, the symbol of ancient Athens. The color of the city's horizon at sunset.

"Fine." Keeping his hands wide of her, Theo took a deep breath. "We need to talk."

"About what?" She lifted her chin. "Maybe we should talk about that little stunt you just pulled, demanding we get married out of nowhere. *Kissing* me? In front of everyone?"

He looked past the reception hall's long folding tables to the homemade wedding cake surrounded by paper plates and stale-looking mints. A hand-painted banner was spread across the back wall, anchored by cheap, drooping balloons. *Congrats, Emmie and Harold.*

His jaw set. "You didn't seem to have any problem marrying that old man."

"Harold's a good person," she protested.

"Why, Emmie? Why him?"

"He offered us a home."

"*I* could give you a home," he said. "Several homes around the world. Why didn't you ask me?"

"Because…" She swallowed, then looked away. Finally she met his eyes. "Why are you pretending you want this, Theo? A wife, a child?"

"I'm not pretending."

She gave a low, bitter laugh. "You forget I know you. Even before I worked for you, I saw how you were. I heard you the morning of Nico's wedding, telling him it wasn't too late to make a run for it! And you were the best man!"

Theo licked his lips. "You heard?"

"I was her maid of honor. I was standing right there. I might have been invisible to you, but…"

"You weren't invisible." He remembered that day, Nico and Honora's wedding on the beach. "You were pretty, in that dress. For once you weren't smothered in the ugliest clothes you could find." His gaze lingered on her lumpy, out-of-date wedding gown, and her cheeks went red.

"You despise the idea of marriage. Why would you ask me?"

Theo looked away, at the arched windows overlooking the courtyard. How to explain something he couldn't even understand himself?

"You're right. I've always avoided commitment," he said haltingly. "In every love affair I've had, I was always planning my exit beforehand. But with you, that night in Rio…"

She waited.

His eyes met hers. "I wasn't careful."

Now Theo heard her sharp intake of breath. She looked down at her hands, clasped in her lap.

"The mistake was mine," he said quietly. She looked up.

"Is that how you see our baby?" Emmie flared. "As a mistake?"

His heart was galloping strangely. "Yes." He looked at her. "A mistake. But it's one I intend to take responsibility for." Looking away, he said softly, "I won't leave you to struggle alone, like my mother had to."

Silence fell. He'd never spoken about his childhood before. Not to anyone.

Emmie's expression changed. "If you want to be a father to our baby, you can." Her tone was suddenly gentle. "I'll let you see him anytime you want. But…that doesn't mean we need to marry."

"The only way I can truly protect him," he said, lifting his chin fiercely, "is by protecting you. The only way I can commit to him…is by committing to you."

Her eyes widened. She took a deep breath, dropping her gaze again. The sweep of her blackened lashes brushed against her cheek like a butterfly's wing.

Makeup made Emmie look…different. More obviously attractive, rather than the secret beauty she'd been, visible to his eyes alone. Theo wasn't sure he liked it.

The truth was, he didn't like any of this.

Not this cheap reception hall. Not feeling tired and hungry after his crazed overnight rush here from Europe. Not being forced into marriage by the conscience he hadn't known he had.

Not Emmie's badly fitting wedding dress, which showed off the swell of her baby bump and her full breasts, barely contained by tight, straining satin. Her pregnant body, laced into that modestly demure dress, made her look like a sex goddess of fertility no man could resist.

Except you'd no longer have to resist her, a voice whispered. His body tightened. Not once she was his wife.

He could still feel their kiss pouring through him, liquid fire in his veins. His gaze kept returning to her face, to her bruised, reddened lips.

"I'm being rude." She looked back at the closed door to the church. "All my family and friends are probably still waiting, wondering what to do. I'm going to tell them it's all off, and they should go home."

His gaze sharpened. "Emmie—"

"I'm not running away. I'll be back."

After she disappeared through the side door, Theo paced, tapping his foot. His hand went to his pocket for his phone, by habit. Then his stomach growled. He hadn't eaten since yesterday. His eyes fell on the wedding cake on the center table.

Crossing past the humble homespun wedding decorations, he brushed his finger alongside the edge of white frosting on the plate. Buttercream. Delicious. He heard a noise.

A white-haired woman in a flowery dress and big pink hat walked through the far door, saying happily to another woman behind her, "It was the answer to my prayers, I tell you. When Harold—"

They stopped when they saw Theo, standing beside the wedding cake with one finger on the edge of the frosting.

"We're here to tidy up," one of the women blurted out. He gave them a hard, charming smile.

"Later."

"Of course," they stammered and fled, holding their dainty hats.

Licking the frosting off his finger, Theo reached for the decorative knife, intending to cut himself a slice—the cake obviously wouldn't be needed now—when his phone rang.

It was his lawyer, calling to report that the demolition permits had come through for his new property in Greece. Hearing it over the phone wasn't quite as satisfying as it would have been to see it in person, as he'd intended.

Then the man added, "And we finally found the item you've been looking for."

Theo blinked. "Where?"

"At a pawn shop. In Thessaloniki. We'll dispatch it to your office." Pause. "I heard you returned to New York quite quickly, sir. Was there an emergency?"

"I came back to get married." It surprised Theo how easy it was to speak those words.

His attorney, the biggest attack dog at the white-shoe law firm of Jaber, Greenbury and Moire, heard the word *married* and gasped out, "But you got a prenup first, of course, Mr. Katrakis?"

Hearing Theo's sheepish reply to the negative, his attorney whimpered like a Victorian maiden collapsing on a fainting couch.

Hanging up moments later, Theo marveled at his own stupidity. He'd been standing at the altar, ready to marry Emmie. He hadn't even thought about the risk to his fortune.

What was it about her that caused him to lose his mind?

Well, no more. From now on he'd be cold. Cold and smart. He'd convince her to marry him—and to sign a prenup. How to convince her? How to get leverage?

The side door opened, and Emmie walked into the reception hall in a swish of white satin, looking pale but determined. He braced himself to argue, to charm, to persuade. "You're going to marry me, Emmie."

She looked at him.

"Fine," she said suddenly. "I will."

CHAPTER THREE

EMMIE'S HANDS WERE still trembling as the two of them went out into the sunlight as if nothing had happened, nothing at all.

After her startling words—startling to her, if not to him—Theo had given her a searching look, then he'd abruptly said, "I'm hungry. Let's talk over lunch."

Outside the church, the colors of her vibrant Queens neighborhood, tiny restaurants with fragrant, unrecognizable spices, and little shops with cheerful clothing fluttering outside swirled around her in a blurry carousel. She blinked, blinded by the blue sky. Blinded by the decision she'd just made.

"It's over there," Theo said, nodding.

"What is?"

"My bike."

Following his gaze, Emmie saw an expensive motorcycle parked arrogantly in the fire lane halfway down the street, a single helmet hanging from the handlebars. "You expect me to ride that?"

"Why not?"

"How would I even hold on to you? With this belly!"

Theo considered her baby bump, then sighed, reaching into his pocket for his phone. "I'll call Bernard."

Bernard Oliver was Theo's chauffeur in New York. But it would take at least thirty minutes for him to drive to Queens. And between them and the motorcycle, she saw clusters of her neighbors and friends in festive hats and their best jackets still filing out of the front steps of the church. Any moment now, they'd turn and see her and Theo at the corner.

She had no intention of spending a half hour answering questions from neighbors. Or letting them see her picked up by Theo's chauffeured Rolls-Royce.

As Theo started to walk ahead, she grabbed his arm. "Let's wait at my apartment. It's not far. We can walk."

His aquiline nose scrunched. "Walk?"

She snorted a laugh. For a man who spent countless hours in boxing gyms and ran marathons, it was hilarious how scandalized he was by the idea of a short walk down the street.

"Yes, walk." She tugged his hand. "Come on."

Emmie dropped his hand as soon as they turned and started walking. It was too hard to touch him. It did strange things to her. Not just her body but her heart.

The kiss he'd given her was still burning through her, from her fingertips to her hair to her toes. That kiss had been so shocking, so overwhelming, it had given her strength to say something the powerful Theo Katrakis almost never heard.

No.

She'd been scared to marry him, scared that he'd end up seducing her body and pillaging her soul, leaving her nothing but an empty husk for the rest of her life.

But when Emmie had gone back alone into the church, something made her change her mind and decide to marry Theo after all.

She'd found her father alone. He'd already told the guests no wedding would happen today so they might as well leave. He'd told his sons they'd already done what they could for Emmie, and they should leave and let the two lovebirds sort themselves out.

But Karl himself had lingered, just in case his daughter needed support. So when Emmie returned, she'd found him alone. They had spoken quietly in a half-shadowed, empty chapel.

"I can't marry him, Dad," she said bleakly. "He'll never love me."

"But you think you could love him?"

She felt a lump in her throat. "Yes."

Her father looked down at the patterns of red and blue and yellow light from the stained glass, pooling against the cool flagstones. Then he lifted his head.

"Your mother was pregnant with you when I married her. You knew that."

She bit her lip. They'd never talked about it. She nodded reluctantly. "I was born six months after your wedding date, so it wasn't hard to figure out."

Karl gave a crooked smile. "Margie didn't love me, either. Not then. She said no the first three times I proposed to her." He ducked his head to surreptitiously wipe his eyes. "When she finally said *yes*, I vowed to make her happy. And I think I did."

"Of course you did." It was startling to think of her romantic, idealistic mother ever not wanting to marry her father. Emmie put a comforting hand on his shoulder. "Mom loved you with all her heart."

"It took a while." He gave her a watery smile, then sobered. "If she hadn't said *yes*, your brothers would never have been born. We would never have been a family."

The thought of that had been so awful, imagining her family disappearing, that Emmie caught her breath.

Her father tilted his head. "If you think you could love Katrakis, well, that's a start, isn't it? And as for him loving you…" His voice trailed off as he gave her a warm smile, his eyes gleaming suspiciously in the dim light. "How could he not? Just give him time."

Time. Emmie didn't think any amount of time could ever make Theo Katrakis love anyone. But in the time it took for her to say farewell to her father and walk back through the side door into the reception hall, Emmie changed her mind.

She would marry Theo. She couldn't imagine not giving her own baby what she'd had: a happy childhood, in spite of all their money worries and the agony of her mother fighting cancer for ten years. How could she possibly justify saying *no*? Her baby's happiness mattered more to Emmie than her own.

And as for her fear of loving Theo—

Why, it was simple, she thought suddenly as she followed him down the street now. Their marriage just needed a few conditions.

One of those conditions would be that their baby would never have siblings, which was a shame. But it would protect her from inevitable heartbreak—especially because she knew she'd never be enough for Theo and he'd soon grow bored with her anyway. So instead of a romantic, passionate partnership, what if, from the beginning, they strove instead for a deep friendship, based on mutual respect? And trust. Trust most of all.

It was the only way to make their marriage endure.

And yet…

Emmie's memory lingered on that kiss of pure fire he'd given her at the altar. She touched her bruised lips. Her condition would mean there'd be no more kisses, luring her into being reckless, luring her into danger. For the rest of her life.

"Look out."

Theo's strong arm suddenly blocked her path. A beat-up car honked loudly as it whizzed past.

Emmie gasped, realized she'd almost stepped into traffic on the street.

With her center of gravity already so off-kilter, she stumbled back, staggering in her tight mermaid skirt, falling back to the sidewalk—

Theo caught her. As their eyes locked, her white veil was caught by the breeze, whirling around them, lifting upward.

Sunlight frosted his dark hair, framing him with blue sky, making his black eyes luminous. She felt the strength of his body against hers, his powerful chest beneath his snug black T-shirt. The shape and power of his thickly muscled arms beneath her hands.

Her gaze fell to his mouth, and she shivered, breathless with sudden longing…

No!

"Pull me up," she gasped. Struggling, she said hoarsely, "Let me go!"

Wordlessly, he set her on her feet. Cheeks hot, she ducked her head, turning to point at a two-story building on the next corner. "That's it."

Careful not to touch him, she led him past the street-level store emblazoned with old neon from her grandfather's day in loopy cursive lettering: *Swenson and Sons Plumbing*. They reached a nondescript door. Typing in the security code, she led him up the stairs to the three-bedroom apartment where her family had always lived.

"Come in," she said. "It'll only take me a minute to change."

"I'll call Bernard and tell him where…" Theo's voice trailed off as he looked around the living room.

Following his gaze, Emmie saw their cozy, too-small home in a new light. It suddenly looked shabby and cluttered. In the mad scramble before the wedding that morning, the sofa bed where her brother Joe slept had been left a mess of tangled sheets. Dirty clothes from various brothers were strewn over the floor. The kitchen table was covered with piles of empty pizza boxes from last night's dinner, with yesterday's dirty dishes stacked in the sink.

Her cheeks went hot as she followed his gaze.

"I didn't have time to cook last night or tidy up as usual," she stammered. "I was busy with the wedding cake…"

"You made that? Yourself?" Theo's dark eyebrows rose, then he licked his lips. "It was good."

"How do you know?"

Not answering, Theo looked around. "You do the cooking and cleaning for your family," he said slowly, "as well as supporting them financially?"

She stiffened, sensing some criticism of her father. She said defensively, "My family's had a hard time since my mother died—"

"Even before that, you were sending your father most of your paycheck." When she jolted in surprise, Theo tilted his head in amusement. "Do you think I didn't know why you first agreed to work for me?"

Emmie ducked her head, embarrassed. "There were medical bills," she mumbled. "My father's hopeless with anything that doesn't require a hand tool, and my brothers, well—" she smiled weakly "—they wouldn't see a mess if they tripped on it."

"I see." He turned away, looking from the dated, worn furniture to the sparkling-clean windows and old carpet beneath her brothers' discarded clothes, which still had lines from the vacuum cleaner she'd used yesterday morning. Faded photographs, school photos, and black-and-white images of her grandparents lined the walls, covering faded wallpaper.

She flinched a little. She could only imagine what he was thinking. Theo Katrakis could have his pick of gorgeous, glamorous women, heiresses, royalty, movie stars. Was he already regretting the surprise pregnancy that had forced him to propose marriage to a plain, plump nobody from Queens?

She turned away. "Wait here. It'll just take me a moment to pack."

"Don't bother. You won't need anything."

Emmie turned back to him. "What do you mean? Won't we live at your penthouse after we're married?"

He looked over her wedding dress. "Tell me you're not planning to wear *that* again."

"No," she said, insulted by his obvious opinion of her mother's gown. Even if she herself had been thinking it was ugly earlier, that didn't give him the same right.

Theo shook his head. "Then, there's nothing for you to pack. *Especially* not those bargain-bin pantsuits."

They'd been more than a bargain. She'd gotten the suits used from a thrift store for five dollars each. But he didn't need to know that. She lifted her chin. "Maybe I *like* those bargain pantsuits. Did you ever think of that?"

His dark eyes challenged her. "Do you?"

She glared at him, then sighed. "No. Not really. But I have better things to think about and better ways to spend money."

"I thought so. That all changes now. You'll need an entirely new wardrobe as my wife."

"Why?" she said suspiciously. "What do you expect me to do?"

Theo's lips curved. "Be at my side at parties, charity balls, dinners with presidents and royalty." Ticking off the items with his fingers, he tilted his head thoughtfully. "Be the hostess of my homes around the world."

Worse and worse. Emmie had always told herself that her plain appearance didn't matter, not as long as she was clean and tidy and competent. Her boss was the important one, not her. But that was when she'd been his secretary. As his wife…

She shuddered. There was no way she could compete with socialites and debutantes!

Theo stroked his chin, watching her as he continued. "You'll be a leader of society," he mused. "A noted taste-maker."

She stiffened at the wicked gleam in his eye.

"In that case," she responded tartly, "the style next season will be whatever's on final clearance at Goodwill."

He snorted, then came closer. Reaching out, Theo smoothed back a long tendril of her hair.

"Give your new life a chance," he said softly. His dark eyes fell to her mouth. "It might be fun."

Oh, no. She wasn't going to let *that* happen, ever again. The kiss he'd given her at the altar still consumed her. Just his touch on the sidewalk, when he'd caught her in his arms to keep her from falling, had reverberated through her body. Nervously, she turned away.

"I'll be just a minute," she said again and fled down the hall to her bedroom, closing the door behind her.

The tiny bedroom, barely bigger than a closet, still had the travel posters of France and Greece she'd put on the walls as a teenager, long before her mother got sick. Old novels still lined the single shelf on the wall, beside a few beloved stuffed animals from her childhood. Her grandmother's homemade quilt covered her twin bed.

Emmie bit her lip. There was no way she'd let Theo see this—the bedroom of a teenager, a decade old, still frozen in time. Turning away, she grabbed an old duffel from beneath her bed and packed a few precious things, photo books, her stuffed bunny from childhood, tiny onesies she'd already bought for her coming baby. After a moment of thought, she decided to leave the secretarial pantsuits behind. He was right. There was no way Mrs. Theo Katrakis could dress like that. She tossed in some underwear and socks, a few stretchy T-shirts and maternity shorts and some shoes. That was it.

Taking off her wedding dress and kicking off her three-inch white pumps, she exhaled, relieved to leave the hot, constricting clothing behind. She spread her mother's gown carefully on her quilt. She'd have to arrange for it to be dry cleaned and packed away.

She pulled a loose cotton sundress over her ungainly body and stuck her feet into flip-flops. Going to the small shared bathroom, Emmie washed the makeup off her face and pulled all the bobby pins out of the bun, letting her hair fall in soft waves over her shoulders.

She felt like she was free, like she could breathe again.

As long as she didn't think about the man she was about to marry. And what he'd say when he heard about her three conditions of marriage:

First, that they'd live in New York.

Second, that he'd help her family with anything they needed.

And third, that they'd never sleep together again. Ever.

* * *

Theo's eyes widened as Emmie returned to the cramped living room of her family's second-floor apartment.

That hideous wedding dress and veil were gone. Emmie now wore a simple sleeveless white cotton sundress and flip-flops. Her face was bare of makeup, her dark blond hair long over her shoulders. His gaze unwillingly lingered on the way it brushed over her collarbones and soft skin.

"Forget it," he said abruptly into his phone. "We'll find our own way. Just pick up the Ducati."

"Who was that?" she asked as he hung up. She was struggling with the handles of a duffel bag that looked fifty years old. Coming around the sofa, he plucked it from her hands.

"Bernard," he answered. "He says there's some politician at the UN choking traffic. He's stuck in congestion by the Midtown Tunnel."

She tilted her head, smiling, and he thought how pretty she was when her violet-blue eyes glowed like that. "So how are you thinking we'll get to Manhattan? Taxi? Rideshare?"

"Sit in the sticky back seat of some stranger?" He shuddered. Setting down the duffel, he typed a search on his phone.

"Subway?" she suggested. "The bus?"

"Bus." He looked up, aghast, then saw her teasing grin. She clearly thought he was being rather silly, which he supposed he was, at least when it came to walking long city blocks or being packed like a sardine into mass transit. But his year living on the streets of Athens at fifteen, trudging sidewalks looking for food or work, trying to slouch in the back rows of buses and train stations long enough to sleep, had been enough for his lifetime. Not that he'd ever tell

anyone about that. Turning back to his phone, Theo said, "There's a car dealership two blocks from here."

Emmie's nose wrinkled. "I know. The gentrification is getting ridiculous. Some of my neighbors tried to fight it, but…where are you going?"

"I'm walking there." He paused to let that sink in. He didn't want to be too predictable. His gaze fell to her belly beneath her loose sundress. "Do you want to wait here? I can come back and pick you up."

"I can walk two blocks," she said dryly. "I just didn't know *you* could."

Carelessly lifting the bag with one hand, he flashed her a sharklike grin. "I'm willing to suffer for a good cause."

As they walked side by side down the lively block, Emmie kept glancing at him through her lashes, as if she were trying to work up to something.

So was he. Theo had no idea how to convince her to sign the prenuptial agreement that would be waiting for them at his penthouse beside their lunch spread. But she had to sign it. His attorney had been very definite about that.

"No prenup, no marriage," he'd insisted to Theo on the phone. "Do you understand, Mr. Katrakis? Do I need to remind you what happened to Bill Gates? Jeff Bezos?" He'd paused. "Robert Romero?"

Theo still shivered at the memory. It was true Bezos and Gates had lost a tidy bundle after prenup-free divorces, but at least those marriages had been long and their wives had helped create those fortunes.

Robert Romero was something else. The self-made frozen-foods tycoon had married a twenty-one-year-old waitress, only to have her file for divorce when they returned from their honeymoon. With her lawyer's help, she'd taken most of the man's fortune. Romero had ended up destitute, shamed, mocked; he died of a heart condition six months later. Whether his heart was broken from losing love or his fortune was an open question.

Mae Baker Romero, the young ex-wife, still lived in a high-rise not too far from Theo's, in a swanky penthouse overlooking Central Park. Called Killer by her friends, she often appeared in gossip columns, flashing her big, bright smile and even bigger and brighter diamonds.

Theo shuddered. Every wealthy bachelor in New York knew the story of Robert Romero.

But how could he convince Emmie to sign the prenup, without her feeling insulted and telling him to forget the whole thing? How could he be diplomatic enough to soften the blow, and seduce, and persuade?

He slanted a sideways glance at her.

In bed, he thought. Obviously. When she was close— hell, even when she'd been thousands of miles away—it was difficult for Theo to think of anything but making love to her. He'd made shocking mistakes because his brain ceased working beneath the onslaught of his desire.

Surely, Emmie had the same problem with him.

Surely?

He recalled how she'd trembled beneath his kiss, her hands gripping him tight. When he'd released her, she'd looked up at him like someone newly woken from a dream. That decided it.

Bed.

Bed, his body agreed fervently.

Walking together through the neighborhood, they arrived at the small used-car dealership about fifteen minutes later. It only took five minutes for Theo to select the best on the lot, a pristine cherry-red 1971 Barracuda convertible. It would be a nice addition to his vintage collection, he thought, as well as quick transportation back to Manhattan. He reached for his wallet.

"No," Emmie said.

Theo frowned, turning to her. The salesman stared at the credit card in his hand intently, vibrating like a dog waiting for a particularly choice bit of meat to drop to the floor. "What do you mean *no*?"

"I'm not getting in that thing." She looked at the low convertible doubtfully. "Even if I could lower myself into the seat, I'd never get up again."

"You'll be fine—"

"Forget it."

As they glared at each other, he suddenly missed the old days when he could override her, when he was demonstrably, undoubtedly the boss.

But even then, sometimes they'd battled, usually when she'd decided to stand her ground in order to prevent him from doing something foolish. Like when his private jet had landed for emergency repairs in Florida and he'd nearly bought thousands of acres of swampland out of sheer boredom. Or the time he'd nearly sold an expensive Tokyo property for a single yen because he'd been annoyed his favorite noodle shop was closed.

On second thought, maybe he should let her win this one. Even if it was damned irritating. Setting his jaw, he demanded, "What exactly do you have in mind?"

Her expressive eyes shifted past him on the car lot, and she smiled. "That."

CHAPTER FOUR

THE JUNE AFTERNOON had grown hot and humid by the time they arrived at his gleaming Manhattan high-rise on the southern edge of Central Park. As Theo pulled the clunky vehicle to the curb, the doorman hurried forward, scowling.

"Hey, you can't park that here—" The young man drew back, shocked. "Mr. Katrakis?"

Theo muttered something under his breath, his jaw tight. Emmie glanced at him with amusement as he put the three-year-old minivan into Park. He was scowling, but driving a minivan for the first time was a well-known test and trial for any red-blooded male. Her smile lifted.

"And—Miss Swenson!" The doorman blinked in surprised recognition as he slid open her door. His jaw dropped as he saw the shape of her pregnant belly beneath her sundress. He stammered, "Er—is it still Miss Swenson?"

"Um…yes." Her cheeks got a little hot, even as she told herself she had nothing to be ashamed of.

"Not for long," Theo said flatly as he yanked her small duffel from the minivan's rear with one hand. "We're going to be married."

The doorman looked speechless, then overjoyed. "Congratulations to you both! Mazel tov! A baby—and married!" Blinking, he looked back at the minivan. "I guess that explains it."

Theo's scowl deepened.

"Just tell Bernard to find a place for it, Arthur," he said and tossed him the key, which the young man caught mid-air.

"Will you keep it?" Emmie asked as she followed Theo inside the grand foyer of the high-rise.

He shrugged. "It served its purpose." Glancing back through the window at the street, he gave a sudden impish grin. "Maybe Arthur would like it as his Christmas tip."

As their footsteps echoed over the marble floor, she snorted a laugh. Trust Theo to think of something like that. His good deeds were impulsive, almost always by accident. "He's a little young for a minivan, don't you think?"

"So am I," he said darkly as they entered the private elevator. The door slid closed, and he looked at her. "But it was what you wanted. Were you comfortable on the ride?"

"Yes," she said honestly.

Reaching out, he smoothed back a tendril of her blond hair. "Then, I suppose we can keep it."

Looking up into his black eyes, Emmie shivered, and it wasn't just from the elevator's blast of air-conditioning. She felt something suddenly tremble deep inside her. Was it from the way he'd put her needs over his own in choosing the car? His gentle touch as he smoothed her hair? Or maybe just his casual use of the word *we*?

Whatever it was, Emmie couldn't—wouldn't—let herself be seduced by it. She turned away, stiffening her shoulders. When the elevator door slid open with a ding, she bolted out.

With its high-ceilinged rooms and three spacious terraces, his multi-million-dollar triplex penthouse sprawled across the entire fifty-second and fifty-third floors of the building, equal parts beautiful and cold.

Not just cold in temperature, either, she thought, glancing up at the jagged crystal chandelier of the foyer. Taking a deep breath, she hurried into the cavernous great room, notable for its lack of color and Spartan furniture. The penthouse's design had been done by a famous interior decorator last year. Emmie had organized it herself at her boss's demand, but to her, the result was chilly, a museum of modern art that might be impressive to outsiders and *Architectural Digest* but was utterly unsupportive of the vibrant chaos of actual human lives.

There was no comfort in Theo's home. Nothing but hard sofas that hurt your back to sit in, framed splatters of gray and black on the walls, and cutting-edge technological interfaces running lights, shades, entertainment, security and the rest.

It was impersonal, too. No photographs of family or proof Theo had ever had one. No clutter. No scattered detritus of hobbies, like her brothers' dusty guitars or her father's pile of hardcover thrillers. No pets. No messes. No inconvenient feelings of any kind.

Just as Theo preferred.

And yet she'd just promised to marry him?

Emmie swallowed, trying to calm the sudden rapid beat of her heart. It would be just a partnership, she told herself. Like they'd had before. She'd never let herself love him again. Maybe she'd let herself care just a little, just the amount that was appropriate since he was her baby's father. But no more than that. So what that he'd bought her a minivan? It meant nothing. Buying things was easy for Theo Katrakis. He threw his money around so that no one would ever notice he never put his heart into anything.

At least he hadn't until he'd stormed her wedding that morning and demanded she marry him instead.

Emmie's eyes fell on Theo's muscular back in the snug-fitting black T-shirt as he walked ahead of her, hearing the echo of his motorcycle boots and slap of her own flip-flops on the concrete floor. As his secretary, she'd previously only visited his home in a professional capacity, wearing a skirt suit and three-inch pumps. She'd typed out his orders and instructions on her tablet, or written in shorthand on a yellow legal pad, working long hours to make Theo's life easier, to make it frictionless, in conjunction with Wilson and with Mrs. Havers, the live-out staff.

Now Emmie was slouching through here in a sundress and flip-flops, coming for lunch, like a guest. No. More than that.

Pregnant with his baby. His future wife.

What had she gotten herself into?

Theo's butler stood waiting for them calmly in the two-story great room, in front of a wall of shining glass windows facing the terrace, and beyond that, the wide view of the park and surrounding city.

"Mr. Katrakis. Welcome home."

Wilson seemed imperturbable as ever in his black suit, the penthouse immaculately clean and ready, as if his boss hadn't just appeared with scant warning after seven months' absence.

The butler's eyes warmed when he saw Emmie. "Miss Swenson. I am pleased to see you're back…" Then his gaze fell to her pregnant belly, clearly visible beneath her white sundress. His eyes actually flickered. A first. Clearing his throat, he said only, "Lunch is on the terrace, sir. Along with the paperwork from your lawyer."

"Good."

"What paperwork?" Emmie asked, but Theo only turned away. "Nice to see you, Wilson," she called, then hurried to follow Theo through the sliding glass doors and out onto the terrace.

Outside was as ascetic in decor as inside, with only a few carefully placed tables and chairs. Stark planters with perfectly clipped greenery separated the terraces into separate spaces, for parties. A clear plexiglass railing, sturdy and bulletproof, revealed every inch of the jaw-dropping view of Central Park and New York City.

In the center of the largest terrace was the crown jewel, a grand dining table for twelve, beneath a pergola that seemed entirely constructed of greenery, white flowers and tiny white lights laced through the foliage.

Turning, Theo stood waiting beside the long table beneath the shade, holding out a chair. She quickened her pace.

"Thanks," she said awkwardly, letting him move her chair up after she sat. Theo had certainly never done *that* when she was his secretary.

Emmie looked at the delicious lunch spread across the table and hardly knew where to begin. Roast beef and turkey sandwiches on a platter, made with Mrs. Havers's fresh-baked baguettes; baby greens with walnuts and blueberries and balsamic dressing; juicy watermelon and red strawberries; salty home-fried chips; chocolate chip cookies for dessert, so warm the chocolate was still oozing from the buttery crust.

Sitting beside her, Theo poured a glass of water from the glass carafe and silently handed it to her.

Taking the glass, Emmie drank deeply and immediately felt refreshed by the cold, sparkling water. It occurred to her that she hadn't had anything to eat in hours, since last night really, when she'd forced down half a piece of cold pizza. She'd been too busy to eat, frantically decorating her wedding cake. That morning, she'd been too nervous, scared that her impending marriage to Harold Eklund was a big mistake.

Now, her appetite returned full force. She loaded her plate, and each thing tasted even better than the last, from the sweet-tart fruit to the crispy chips and tangy salad. She washed it all down with juice and more water, then dug in to her third sandwich, with the savory cheddar and roast beef with Dijon on chewy homemade bread.

Then her gaze fell on the clipped stack of papers, perhaps thirty pages of small-font type, sitting on the far end of the long table. Swallowing the last bite of her sandwich, she squinted. "What's that?"

Theo calmly finished his glass of water, washing down his own plate of food which he'd already refilled several times. "Our prenuptial agreement."

Her mouth fell open. She said, faltering, "Prenup?"

He tilted his head. "Surely you, of all people, knew there'd be one."

After all her time working as his secretary, seeing Theo Katrakis fight for the best deal and always make sure he could never, ever get screwed by an opponent, Emmie should have expected it. But she hadn't.

She stared at the prenup.

Resting on top of the paperwork was an expensive pen, edged with twenty-four-karat gold. It was the pen Theo always used, signing with a flourish, when he felt he'd made a particularly ruthless deal. Her mouth went dry.

He smiled, his white teeth glinting in the sun. "You don't mind, do you?"

Emmie had talked herself into settling for a marriage of

partnership if she couldn't have love, but it seemed even that had been too much to hope for.

So much for trust. Theo was already planning their divorce.

"I spoke with my lawyer," he said casually, eating the last chip from his plate, "and I'm afraid I can't marry you without it."

Turning, she stared out past the pergola to the vast greenery of Central Park and distant skyline, sharp against the blue sky.

"Emmie?"

"Fine." Standing up, she grabbed the prenup and returned to her chair. "I'll read it."

She read every word, carefully. She felt him getting restless as the minutes passed. Like many rich, powerful men, Theo disliked unfilled time. He looked down at his phone, reading and typing with his thumbs, fidgeting in his chair.

Emmie took her time, licking a fingertip as she turned the pages, occasionally marking something in a margin for her own memory.

"It's fine for you to get your own attorney to look it over, if you wish," Theo said finally.

"It's not exactly hard to understand," she said and continued to placidly read in the shade of the pergola as Theo got up and paced the terrace. Finally, she looked up.

"All right. I'll sign it."

He returned quickly to the table, his handsome face relieved. "Good. I'll get Wilson to witness, and we can have a judge here to perform the ceremony in—"

"But I have a few conditions of my own," she said.

Theo sat in his chair, leaning back to cross his ankle over his knee, his body language relaxed, friendly now he'd gotten his way. He smiled. "I would expect nothing less."

"Just three small things."

"I'm all ears."

Emmie took a deep breath. "First. Our primary domicile will be in New York City."

He tilted his head with a frown. "I travel constantly for work. You know that better than anyone."

She looked at him evenly. "And the baby and I may travel with you…sometimes. But I want to raise our child in one place, a real home. Not drag him from place to place living out of a suitcase like some backpacker on a gap year."

Theo set both feet back on the floor, sitting up straight, all his earlier casual friendliness gone now that there was a threat to his future convenience.

"Why here? Why not Aspen, St. Moritz, London?" he asked, listing the settings of his other multi-million-dollar residences. "Or even Greece? I just bought something there today…"

"You might own houses in those places, but they're not home."

"Home can be anywhere we are," he challenged. "We could live happily in five-star hotels in Paris, Tokyo, Sydney. Why not—" his dark eyes lifted to hers "—Rio?"

She shivered. No. She wasn't going to think about that night in Rio.

"New York is my home," she said quietly. She clasped her hands in her lap so he couldn't see them trembling. "My family is thirty minutes away. My friends live here. My *best* friend. And yours," she added, thinking of Honora and Nico.

His jaw tightened. He was clearly irritated at her persistence. As his secretary, she'd always done what he wanted.

"Fine," he bit out. "Your second condition?"

Emmie lifted her chin. "I want your permission to help

my family as I see fit. Don't worry, nothing crazy," she rushed to say as he raised his eyebrows. "Just enough to replace what I do in Dad's business and at home. Some money for his retirement. Maybe some of my brothers could go to community college or learn a trade, since I'm not sure they're all interested in plumbing." Another reason the business had been doing so badly the last few years.

"Very well." Theo's handsome face was cold, unreadable. "And the last condition?"

This was the hard one. Emmie took a deep breath.

"I release you from all the adultery clauses in the prenup." She drummed her fingers nervously over the pile of papers. "As far as I'm concerned, you can sleep with whomever you want."

Theo gasped, his eyes wide. She'd never seen him look so shocked.

"What?" he stammered. "Why?"

"Marriage lasts a lifetime. Or it should. And it would be unreasonable for me to expect you to never have sex again. So my final condition of marrying you is—sleep with anyone you want." Emmie lifted her gaze to his. "As long as it's not with me."

Be married to Emmie and never make love to her?

Had she lost her mind?

Theo set his jaw. Taking a deep breath, he tried to control the pounding of his heart and make his voice sound reasonable. "You're angry I want you to sign a prenup."

"No," Emmie said. Looking up at the pergola's greenery and white blooms, she sighed with a wistful smile. "You are who you are."

Theo had always tried to take pride in that, so why did

her words make him feel like he'd somehow let her down? Worse—like he'd let *himself* down?

Stubbornly, he pushed the feeling aside. "So you're trying to punish me for being practical and logical? *You*, of all people? Because that's all a prenup is. A logistical plan."

"Why would I punish you for that?" she agreed sardonically. Dappled sunlight caught gold and strawberry glints in her dark blond hair. "I love that you're already planning our divorce."

He ground his teeth. "I'm not…" Then he realized that a prenuptial agreement was, by definition, laying the groundwork for their divorce. He took a breath. "You must see that any man in my position has no choice but to ask for this. I'd be a fool otherwise."

"And you're not a fool."

"Exactly."

"Because you earned your money the hard way, all on your own."

"Yes."

"And it wouldn't be fair if you were forced to share *your* money with some nobody ex-wife, who'd done absolutely nothing but raise your child."

"Uh…" he said, sensing danger. He changed tactics. "So you're just trying to delay signing it? By coming up with a crazy idea of celibacy that would only hurt us both?"

"I'm not delaying anything. I'll sign right now." Brushing through the pages, she marked it up with her pen and handed it to him. "Here. Call in Wilson to witness."

Looking down, Theo saw she'd crossed out the clause that would have paid her millions in any divorce caused by his adultery. "You can't be…" As he read further, his eyes widened. He looked up triumphantly. "You made a mistake."

"Did I?"

"You forgot to cross out the same penalty if *you* cheat on me." He snorted. "You can't mean that you'd encourage me to sleep with every woman in the world with no problem, while if you so much as kiss another man, I could divorce you and you wouldn't get a penny, not even if we'd been married thirty years. How would that be fair?"

"It wasn't a mistake," she said serenely.

"What?"

Emmie shrugged. "I'm not going to cheat on you. For me, marriage vows are sacred."

Insinuating that they weren't sacred for him? He ground his teeth. "So let me get this straight. You're telling me to sleep around, while you're planning to remain chaste as a virgin for the rest of your life."

Her cool violet eyes met his. "For the rest of my life."

Theo leaned forward in his chair, furious.

"Why, Emmie?" he ground out. "Tell me why."

She looked down at her clasped hands in the lap of her white sundress, resting close to the swell of her belly. "I don't have to explain."

"You're wrong. I deserve to know." He licked his dry lips. "It can't be…can't…"

It couldn't be that she didn't want him.

Could it?

A hot breeze blew across the rooftop terrace, ruffling the papers on the table, swaying the flowers and vines woven above. Several pages of the prenup broke free from the paper clip and scuttered across the terrace. Rising, he went to pick them up.

All he could think about was their kiss that morning, how he'd felt her respond in his arms, rising like the center of a storm.

And in Rio—

After weeks of work closing a development deal, he and Emmie had both been exhausted. When she'd sighed that they never had time to see anything but the job site and conference rooms in the cities they visited, Theo had decided to prove her wrong. So after they'd closed the deal, he'd called in a favor and taken her to Mount Corcovado above the city after the site was officially closed for the night. The two of them were alone at the base of Rio's most famous symbol, the massive Cristo Redentor statue, lit up in the darkness.

"It's beautiful," she had whispered, shivering. Seeing she was cold, even in the warm night, he'd put his jacket over her, and together they'd looked out at the lights of the city, scattered islands and moonlight over Guanabara Bay.

Then he'd paused, his hands still around her. He felt a tropical breeze blow against his overheated skin. Their eyes caught in the moonlight, and feeling like he was in a dream he'd lowered his mouth to hers.

Kissing Emmie at the top of Mount Corcovado, with Rio sparkling like stars beneath them, he'd felt dazed, drugged with desire. They'd wordlessly returned to the waiting sedan and their hotel on Ipanema Beach. The whole time, his brain was shrieking that he had to stop this, that it was madness, that if he didn't stop it would destroy the best relationship he'd ever had.

Because after nearly a year and a half together, they'd become more than boss and secretary. Working together, day and night, sharing setbacks and triumphs, he'd come to consider Emmie a friend, and those he let even slightly past his guard were few.

But when they'd reached his hotel suite, she'd lifted her

violet-blue eyes, hazy with desire, and licked her swollen lower lip.

"Kiss me," she'd whispered.

And he'd been lost. He didn't care that he was her boss. Even if it destroyed him and burned his entire fortune to ash in that moment, he would still have taken her. As the warm wind blew from the open balcony, twisting the curtains, he'd possessed her as his own and, discovering her virginity, known such pure and perfect ecstasy he thought he might die in her arms.

And in some ways, he had.

Emmie had disappeared the next morning, after she'd gotten the awful phone call from her father. He'd expected her to return after the funeral, but instead, she'd called him and said she was never coming back.

And since Rio, Theo had had no interest in other women, no matter how beautiful. What supermodel, what mere *actress*, could possibly compare to the glory he'd known in the arms of his secretary that forbidden night?

The night they'd conceived a child...

Now, Theo's gaze lingered on her bare pink Cupid's-bow lips, falling unwillingly to the swell of her breasts overflowing the modest neckline of her sundress. His body was taut with desire.

And yet Emmie wanted to refuse him her bed? She wanted to push him into the arms of *other women*?

"Whatever your reason, it can't be you don't want me," he said hoarsely. "I know you do. Just as I want you."

Emmie shifted in her chair. The shade from the pergola's foliage left patterns of light and dark against her skin, the curve of her cheekbone, the sweep of her lashes that seemed to tremble before she turned away, looking out at the Manhattan skyline.

"Wanting you isn't the problem," she said finally.

"Then, what is?"

Rising to her feet, Emmie turned away, walking toward the clear railing of the terrace's edge. She looked out onto the view of Central Park and sun-drenched blue sky. Rising to his feet, he followed her.

"Emmie," he said softly, coming up behind her. "What is it?"

She whirled around. "I'm afraid, all right?"

"Afraid?" He was bewildered. "Of what? Of me?"

"Afraid..." Emmie lifted her gaze, her lovely face anguished. "If I sleep with you again," she whispered, "I'm afraid you'll break my heart."

"Break your...?" Theo staggered back, his brow furrowed in shock. That would have to mean... "You can't be saying that you...love me?"

"I know, right?" She looked away. "What kind of fool would that make me?"

He exhaled in relief. She'd scared him for a second. Relieved, he gave a low laugh. "We both know you're too smart for that. You're practical. Modern. You don't do feelings. You're like me. Plus, you know me too well. Remember what you said when I first asked you to work for me?"

She didn't join his laugh. "I said pigs would fly before I could ever love you."

"So," he tilted his head, "how could I ever break your heart?"

Emmie looked down at her flip-flops.

"No matter what you might think right now, Theo, we both know you can't commit to one woman for long. You can't bear to be tied down. There's no way you could be faithful to one woman for the rest of your life. And no matter how practical I might be," she said softly, "I can't be the lover of a man who won't be true." She looked up. "The only way it won't hurt me is to never sleep with you again. If we can just be partners. Friends."

Theo stared at her, his whole body thrumming with emotion. "You think I can't be faithful?"

Avoiding his eyes, Emmie snorted, shaking her head. It was strange to see bitter cynicism on her young face, usually so earnest. "I've never seen you commit to anyone, Theo. Even before I started working for you, I knew you were a playboy. How could I possibly be the woman to tame you?" She looked down at her old sundress, her flip-flops, the chipped pink polish on her toes. "Look at me. And look," she said as she lifted her chin, "at *you*."

Theo shifted his motorcycle boots against the terrace. His black clothes, which had seemed so reasonable on his private jet that morning, were now far too hot in the sun.

Or maybe it was having Emmie so close.

He exhaled. He knew there was some truth to what she said. He'd never been interested in settling down. No, more than that—he'd actively avoided it, at all costs. He knew he was attractive to women, in a thuggish sort of way, just as he knew that he was good at driving and ruthless in business. He used what he had as a tool to get what he wanted, nothing more and nothing less. His face had been given to him by his parents—by the father he'd never known, and the mother he didn't want to remember. He couldn't take credit for his face, apart from the fight that had broken his nose at fifteen.

He could take some credit for his body, due to frequent exercise at boxing gyms. But that was to alleviate stress. A therapist had once told him exercise could help relax him and calm his mind. He'd never gone back to the therapist— he didn't like how she'd tried to pry into things best left buried—but he'd taken her suggestion about exercise. It often helped to pound a punching bag or willing opponent until he was exhausted and covered with sweat. Drinking could also work, if he didn't mind the hangover. And sex, though that often had unfortunate consequence of dealing with a woman begging for his love or attention afterward.

Work was the best distraction of all. Until that night in Rio, it had been the only thing he could always rely on, better than any drug, to help smooth the rough edges of the day and the hollow emptiness in his soul.

Then the night with Emmie had changed everything. For the only time in his life, he'd truly been able to forget everything he wanted to forget in an ecstasy so deep it was almost holy.

And now she wanted to refuse him? She wanted to live as his wife, in his home, raising his child—but deny him her body, pushing him into the cold, unappealing arms of other women?

"You're wrong, Emmie," he said in a low voice. He lifted his eyes to hers. "I can be faithful. I *have been*."

She swallowed. "What are you saying?"

Coming closer, Theo pulled her into his arms beside the railing with all of Central Park and New York City at their feet.

"Since our night together, there's been no one else. *No one.* And I swear to you now—" he searched her gaze fiercely "—if you marry me, for the rest of my life you'll be the only one."

CHAPTER FIVE

CANDLES WERE GLOWING across the penthouse terrace as Emmie took a deep breath and stepped out into the warm summer night.

Another wedding, another day as a bride. But this time was so different. The lights of the city sparkled like diamonds, as above, the moon glowed like a pearl in black velvet.

Holding her arm, her father couldn't speak for the tears in his eyes. Her proud, gruff father openly weeping wasn't the only reason he was almost unrecognizable. His gray hair was sleekly trimmed, and he was dressed in a designer suit, with a new gold watch on his wrist, a gift from her bridegroom.

Emmie had received the upgrade treatment, too. She hardly recognized herself, either, in the short, deceptively simple shift dress that could best be described as quiet luxury: hemline at the knee, cowl neckline, long sleeves with a slight bell shape at the wrist. Her hair had been styled in a soft, elegant chignon, and rather than veiled was adorned with a large white rose. Her makeup was discreet, far more discreet than the enormous pearl studs in her ears—those, too, were a gift from the groom, and she was sure they'd cost a fortune. But not as much as the emerald-cut diamond engagement ring on her left hand, which was big enough to be seen from space.

Her cheeks burned as she and Karl walked past the fifty or so standing guests watching them with big eyes. Theo had hired the most expensive wedding planner in the city and demanded a small, elegant ceremony to be produced in four days. The woman had done as he'd asked, for an exorbitant amount that still made Emmie wince to think of it. It was unreasonable how much he'd spent, to achieve something they could have done quietly and easily by going to the courthouse downtown. But what Theo Katrakis wanted Theo Katrakis got.

She shivered.

Walking ahead of them was Honora Ferraro, her best friend who'd returned from the Caribbean especially to be her one and only bridesmaid. She held a single long-stemmed white rose, matching the seven of them in Emmie's elegant bridal bouquet—exactly seven roses, to symbolize harmony and also the four elements and yin and yang and something else. Emmie had been too distracted to follow the planner's explanation, but she figured she'd take all the luck she could get.

The last few days had been a whirlwind of wedding planning and dress fittings and cake tastings. Other than paying for everything, Theo had been absent, busy at the office, as he said, trying to finish up some loose ends so they could leave to honeymoon at some mysterious location. It had been strange to be sleeping in the guest room of this big penthouse, not quite a wife, not his employee, not even really his guest. But in a few minutes, after they spoke their vows, she would have a new place in the world. She'd be Mrs. Theo Katrakis.

Walking across the terrace to harp music, Emmie tottered on four-inch white strappy sandals. Her gaze rested on her four younger brothers, all looking unusually civilized in sleek designer suits that matched her father's.

Her family was far more thrilled about this wedding than they'd been about her prospective alliance to Harold Eklund four days before. Emmie privately wondered if it was possible Theo had bought them all off.

But then, was she any better?

She was marrying him for their baby's sake, she told herself firmly. Their marriage would be a practical one, a partnership to create a stable home for their child. Beyond that, she didn't give two hoots about Theo's wealth. As long as a family could pay their bills, she'd seen no evidence that a big fortune made anyone happier in life. It sure hadn't given Theo much joy that she could see. And yet he kept chasing it.

No, Emmie didn't care about Theo's fortune. She was no gold digger.

But there would be other benefits she did care about...

She shivered as her eyes fell on her bridegroom, waiting in front of the pergola with the judge and Nico, his best man. Behind them, Manhattan sparkled beneath the sweep of the summer moonlight.

Theo's black eyes met hers.

He was wearing a bespoke tuxedo that fit him to perfection, hand-tailored to the hard angles of his powerfully muscled body. She looked up, dazzled by his masculine beauty. Even the slight crookedness of his nose made him more exotic, so strong, so different.

Her heart was pounding.

Theo had insisted on replacing the line in the prenup that she'd tried to cross out. They'd both signed the original version, which listed financial penalties for adultery—by either party. In spite of her weak protests, he'd seemed utterly confident that he'd soon be able to seduce her.

Emmie shivered, fearing he was right. She wasn't sure how long she could keep him from her bed, or even if she should, when she wanted him just as badly as he wanted her. Even now, just looking at him, her body was fire. She didn't realize she'd licked her lips until she tasted lipstick.

She wanted him.

She always had, from the day they'd met at Honora and Nico's wedding years before, Emmie as maid of honor, Theo the best man. Even though he was a handsome billionaire playboy, and she'd been a chubby, working-class nobody, not remotely pretty or interesting. She'd still wanted him. Desperately. She'd hidden her longing with barbed insults for years.

Now Theo was going to be hers.

No. He'd already been hers, though she had not known it. He'd had no other lover since the night they'd conceived their baby.

He'd had no reason to be faithful. They'd never officially been a couple. Why would a playboy be faithful to a one-night stand?

And yet he had. He'd wanted only her.

Knowing that, how could Emmie resist?

"You're practical," he'd told her. "Modern. You don't do feelings. You're like me."

She wished he was right. That she could simply enjoy sex with her husband, without letting her heart get in the way.

But that wasn't her, and she knew it. She had to resist. *Had to.* Because if she succumbed to her desire, there would be nothing to keep her from falling in love with him all over again. Even though she knew her husband would never, ever love her back.

And she'd be lost...

As they reached the pergola, her father transferred her hand to Theo's, and he kept his large hand wrapped reverently around hers. Emmie looked up at the soft flicker of light playing across her bridegroom's rugged face from the columns of tall white candles.

The vows were spoken. A plain gold band for him, a thin platinum band matching the diamond engagement ring for her. There was nothing religious in the judge's words, and yet this moment held a breathless hush to Emmie as they were united, their lives tied together forever.

Then the judge grinned. "You may kiss the bride."

As the guests standing around them applauded and cheered on the terrace, their noise echoing out into the warm summer night in this sparkling city, Theo lowered his head and kissed her.

And as his lips touched hers, Emmie trembled and was suddenly scared she was already lost.

It was over. He'd done it. They were *married*.

There was no getting out of it now.

As Theo pulled away from the brief kiss, after the judge proclaimed them husband and wife, he looked down at his new bride amid the applause.

Emmie's eyes were luminous, glowing brighter than the candles around them, brighter than the city lights or stars in the darkness above. But he saw something in her expression. Some private grief, some agonized question.

And he felt something tighten painfully in his chest.

"Congratulations, man," Nico said, clapping him on the shoulder. His best man had been a rock through this. That very morning, when Theo had returned to the penthouse at dawn after finding reasons to stay at the office all night, he'd felt cold and clammy and wondered if he was coming down with something.

Fear. He'd been coming down with fear.

Emmie, of course, had no idea of his surfaced doubts. He'd known he couldn't tell her. Their union was already on shaky-enough ground, without him sharing, just hours before their wedding, that he felt sick to the soul at the promise he was about to make.

To love and cherish forever? What was he thinking? No one could promise that. Life was hard and uncertain.

And fidelity? It had been easy to be faithful to her for the last seven months. He hadn't even wanted another woman. But how could he promise that he'd never feel differently? What if he did?

What if Emmie did? What if she—

And it was at that moment he'd realized he was sweating and had picked up his phone blindly, intending to call his pilot and arrange a quick flight to the other side of the world.

But he couldn't do that. He couldn't abandon his unborn son. Not after what Theo himself had gone through when he was young.

So instead, he'd called his best friend—his only close friend, really, aside from Emmie herself. He knew Nico Ferraro had once gone through something similar himself, marrying the granddaughter of an employee in a shotgun wedding—literally—after she surprised him with a pregnancy, knocking on his door in the middle of the night, right before her enraged grandfather showed up with a shotgun, demanding they marry.

But if Theo had secretly hoped that his friend would suggest, as he himself had before Nico's wedding, that it wasn't too late to make a run for it, he'd been disappointed.

Instead, Nico had listened, sympathized and then proceeded to tell stories about how glad he was that he'd married Honora, that the marriage had been the making of him, that he couldn't imagine a life without her or their children.

All very well for him. But from a young age, Theo had seen too much in the world to believe in fairy tales. He'd never believed in any of it—that good always triumphed over evil, that love could last forever, that families could love and protect each other to the end.

The only way to survive in this harsh life was to be strong and alone.

But even knowing this, Theo had found somewhat to his surprise that he couldn't desert his son. So he'd gone through with the wedding. It had taken all his strength to make his lips speak the words.

Now, as Theo turned to face his wedding guests, he was a married man. And looking at his bride's big, nervous eyes, he was wondering if he'd just made the biggest mistake of his life.

"We're so happy for you both." Nico's wife, Honora, was beaming at them. "Our two best friends married? It's a dream come true!"

"I still can't believe you were the father of Emmie's baby all along. Even when I told you she was pregnant by some man in Rio," Nico said, laughing, "you didn't say a word!"

Emmie blushed. "It just happened. We never intended…"

"Yes, we know how that goes," Nico said, exchanging a loving, amused glance with his wife, whose cheeks blushed even redder than Emmie's. Honora turned quickly to her friend.

"Just think, our children will grow up together." She hugged Emmie carefully, so as not to muss her gown. "Our families can take vacations together. The South of France. Italy. Greece."

"Except Theo hates Greece," Nico said, looking at him uncomfortably.

Both women looked at him, startled.

"You do?" Emmie said.

"How could anyone hate Greece?" Honora said.

Theo kept his expression cold. "Actually, I recently bought property on a Greek island."

Nico, who knew only the tiniest bit of Theo's history, looked astonished. "You did?"

Seeing all the other guests waiting to congratulate them, Emmie's family and a few friends from her neighborhood and a whole bunch of his own acquaintances, important society and business people he didn't actually give a damn about, Theo decided he wanted to finish this wedding as quickly as possible. He grabbed Emmie's hand. "We should have our dance."

"Great idea." Nico immediately took his own wife in his arms. "We must take advantage of being on our own tonight. No babies or grandparents to interrupt us."

"Is that your new definition of romance?" Honora teased, but her eyes flashed with love.

Emmie seemed less keen to dance with Theo. "Already?" She looked around. "But we haven't even said hello to all our guests—"

"We can do what we want," Theo said roughly, by which he meant what *he* wanted.

And so, to the despair of the wedding planner, Theo started the dancing an hour ahead of schedule, before the cocktails or hors d'oeuvres had been served, before cake, before even the champagne toast.

As he led her onto the impromptu dance floor on the terrace beneath the moonlight, he tried to ignore the erratic pounding of his heart. It was only when the music started and he pulled her into his arms that he could breathe again.

Yes. When he held Emmie in his arms, her body pressing against his own, the roar in his ears receded, the panic disappeared.

She looked up at him, her eyes bright, her mouth curving up. "You really don't like weddings, do you? Not even your own."

Especially not my own, he wanted to say, but he didn't because that might have hurt her feelings.

So he said brusquely, "I got a phone call right before the ceremony. I need to go into the office."

"What…now?"

"On the way to the airport."

"Fine," she sighed. She glanced at her father and two of her brothers, now smiling at the married couple from the edge of the dance floor. "What did you do to them? I think they now love you more than me."

He said coolly, "You told me you wanted your family taken care of financially, did you not?"

Her eyes focused on him. "Yes?"

"I told them I'd pay for any upgrades the plumbing business needed, and housing for your brothers, as well as for college or trade school for the ones who preferred to branch out on their own."

"You did what?" Her lips parted. "What did my father say?"

"He demanded that I promise to always take care of you and make you happy," he said shortly. Another promise he wasn't sure he'd be able to keep. All these promises he'd spread around. His heart started to pound again.

"We'll both try to be good partners," Emmie said stiffly,

and she looked away, a little wistfully he thought, at Honora and Nico clinging to each other passionately on the dance floor.

Theo looked down at her. In the moonlight, his new wife looked breathtakingly beautiful. The white bloom in her hair gave her the look of a medieval maiden in a pre-Raphaelite painting. The soft white silk dress fit like water running over the swollen curves of her pregnant body.

Turning beneath his gaze, Emmie furrowed her brow, her pretty face turning uncertain. "What is it?" She licked her lips. "Is something wrong?"

The music ended, and he thankfully didn't have to answer. Taking her hand, he led her off the dance floor.

Theo endured the next hour by watching the clock, smiling when required, saying *Thank you for coming* when he was congratulated, speaking directly into his own camera in Greek, sending a video message to Sofia in Paris, telling her he'd see her soon. It was the least he could do, after he'd all but forbidden her to attend his wedding today. She'd cried on the phone when he told her.

But it was better for her to keep her distance. Her life was better without Theo in it. Why couldn't she see that? Hadn't he ruined enough for her?

Pushing thoughts of Sofia away, he focused on listening to Emmie's carefully written, if somewhat stilted, wedding toast. As she teased him about his workaholic ways, causing a ruffle of laughter through the crowd, she also made her deep respect for him clear. By the end of her toast, as she held up her sparkling San Pellegrino, and everyone else held up their Dom Pérignon, Theo felt surprised, touched, but most of all deeply uncomfortable. He knew he didn't deserve praise.

His own toast, spoken off the cuff, certainly made that

clear. He'd simply held up his glass and looked at his bride. "To you!"

Even Nico, normally his most loyal friend, looked a little startled at Theo's obvious lack of preparation or his plain ineptitude.

But for the last few days, Theo had been unable to think of writing his wedding toast to his bride without breaking into a sweat. A pity he couldn't ask Emmie to write it for him, but even he could see that wouldn't be appropriate. As it was, he'd been forced to delegate the task to Edna, the elderly secretary sent to him by an agency after Emmie left—Edna with the dyed black hair who distrusted computers, smelled vaguely of mothballs, and repeatedly called Theo *hon*. Sadly, her attempt at a wedding toast, fusty witticisms cobbled together from some long-dead humorist's book of maxims, was unintelligible.

So he'd had to wing it. If brevity was the soul of wit, *To you!* should have been a wedding toast for the ages.

Unfortunately, his bride didn't seem to see it that way. Her lovely face had fallen.

Not the first time Theo had disappointed her. Definitely wouldn't be the last.

"We should go," he said in a low voice while everyone was still gulping their drinks. "I need to pick something up at the office."

She looked bewildered. "You said we could do it later."

"And now it's later."

Her brow furrowed. "Can't we just send someone for it?"

"I need to do it myself."

"Why?"

"I just do."

"But we haven't even cut the cake. It came from the

best baker in the city…" Then she looked at his face more closely. "All right. Let's go."

Theo blinked, feeling a sense of vertigo at her sudden change. He wondered what she'd seen in his face. He didn't like to think of anyone being able to see into his soul. He told himself it didn't matter, as long as he got what he wanted. Which was getting the hell out of here.

Theo gave discreet orders to his butler, and within five minutes, bride and groom were heading for the car, showered with rice, praise and some good-natured teasing by their guests: "I've never seen anyone so keen to start their honeymoon!"

But once the two of them were sitting in the back of the Rolls-Royce, as Bernard drove them through the dark, empty streets of a late weekday evening in Manhattan, it was suddenly far too quiet for Theo's liking. Especially with their suitcases in the trunk for their honeymoon. He'd picked the location as an act of bravado, a way to prove to himself how far he'd come. But had he? Had he really?

For his whole adult life, he'd managed to contain his emotions, to avoid even having them. But now, for some reason, they were suddenly circling.

Emmie's eyes caught his in the back seat, and he looked away sharply, his heart in his throat.

Normally, he would have thrown himself into work for four days or ten, until he was too exhausted and distracted to feel anything. But he could hardly work now, when he'd insisted on dragging his new bride from their wedding. He couldn't exactly jump out of the car and run a quick ten miles, either.

Only one other stress reliever would do.

His gaze slid sideways to the curve of Emmie's breast. They were married now. Leaving on honeymoon. He didn't believe for a second that Emmie actually intended their marriage to be in name only. She'd enjoyed their night together as much as he had. So either she was lying to him, trying to gain the upper hand in their relationship—good luck with that—or else she was lying to herself for some reason. Either way, it was time to clear the air and fall into bed. He couldn't wait until they arrived at their honeymoon destination. And his private jet did have a bed…

In Midtown, he strode into his office building to get this errand done so they could reach that jet as quickly as possible. Emmie followed in her wedding dress. He greeted the security guard, who took in their attire and smiled.

"Congratulations, sir."

"Thanks for coming—" Catching his automatic response too late, Theo corrected himself. "Er, thanks for keeping an eye on things here."

Upstairs, Theo found his empty office floor and all the unfilled cubicles deathly quiet.

"Why are we here?" Emmie asked behind him. He glanced at her, then without responding, kept walking.

His private office was large, with high ceilings, and a very expensive desk. His company had offices in cities around the world, but New York City was technically his headquarters. Unlocking his safe hidden behind a black-and-white Jackson Pollock painting, he pulled out a small, plainly wrapped package, three inches square. His hand trembled a little as he looked down at it in his palm.

"It's funny to be here." Emmie gave a low laugh as she looked around the office. "So much has changed since I was here last…"

Moonlight from the high arched window flooded his private office, illuminating dappled patterns on her wedding dress and the white rose in her hair, her eyes bright. She looked like an angel. An angel he didn't deserve.

And a sensual one, a divine angel of sin. His gaze fell to her full breasts and belly, straining against the thin white of the silk, and he shuddered. There was no way he could wait until they reached the jet at Teterboro.

Now. He needed her now.

Locking the safe, sliding the painting back over it, he dropped the small package in his jacket pocket. He crossed the office, standing inches away from her, towering over her.

Emmie looked up in the moonlight, and her expression changed. She said brokenly, "Theo—"

But he didn't want to hear arguments or reasons. He didn't want to think at all. After everything he'd endured to do the right thing—marry her—he wanted only to claim his prize.

Pulling her roughly into his arms, Theo kissed her. No soft short kiss, either, like the one he'd given her at their wedding. No.

This kiss was hungry. Dirty. Hard. He plundered her mouth in an intensity of need. She gasped against his lips, and for a moment he felt her hesitate. His grip tightened.

Then she returned his kiss with a desperation that matched his own. A bed, they needed a bed—

The desk. The big desk where they'd spent over a year working together, where for months he'd tried not to notice how beautiful his secretary was, when he'd tried and failed not to desire her. Yes. He'd take her on the desk, right here and now—

Cupping her breasts through the sensuous silk, he deepened the kiss as she trembled in his arms. Reaching beneath the fabric of her bra, he felt the warmth of her skin against his palms and stroked her nipples between his fingers.

Ripping away from the kiss, he lowered his head to one nipple, then the other, savoring the taste as each pebbled in the heat of his wet mouth. He heard her moan and was suddenly so hard his whole body shook with need. He had to have her—now. Pushing her against the desk, he fell to his knees in front of her, yanking up her wedding dress, reaching for her white lacy panties, pushing her thighs apart—

"No," she choked out suddenly, and then, "No!"

Roughly, she shoved him away. Startled, Theo stumbled back. Regaining his balance, he straightened. For a moment, they stared at each other in the shadows, blinking in the moonlight.

"I meant what I said," Emmie said hoarsely. "I'm not going to sleep with you."

Then she slid off the desk and, without a single backward glance, left him standing in the shadows of his office.

He stared at the empty doorway, his heart still pounding, dazed with lust.

Seducing her was going to require more effort than he'd thought.

Theo took a deep breath, gripping his hands against the desk. He wanted her. Badly.

And he would have her. They had their whole honeymoon ahead of them. Seducing his wife was now his one and only goal.

Theo intended to be utterly ruthless.

CHAPTER SIX

Flinging open the blue shutters, Emmie stuck her head out the window and took an invigorating breath of sea-salt air.

Beyond the whitewashed walls of the tiny Greek hotel, which was really just a few guest rooms above a taverna, she could see the sapphire Aegean sparkling in the morning sun.

Past the fishing boats in the bay, she saw a yacht on the horizon. Was it Theo's, coming to collect them? She hoped not.

This sleepy village was off the beaten path, far from Mykonos or Santorini. Lyra was just a small rocky isle with limited ferry service and no nightclubs or mega resorts, with more grazing sheep than tourists. The island had just one village, also named Lyra, with a few scattered two-story hotels, quiet beach coves, and tavernas overlooking the harbor, where fishermen with stubbly beards and low-slung caps brought in that day's catch with nets on their rusted boats.

And it was all so wonderful, so beautiful and glorious, that it made Emmie's heart hurt with joy.

She turned away from the window, back to their small room. The innkeeper's wife had grandly called it the honeymoon suite, but maybe that was because space was so tight in here, honeymooners were the only ones who'd want it. Seeing her husband sleeping in the small bed, her heart twisted as tightly as the sheets tangled at his feet.

They'd slept together last night.

Just *slept*.

She'd barely managed to push him away in New York. Refusing him, when she wanted him just as badly, was the hardest thing she'd ever done. But she couldn't give in, not without falling for him all over again. And he was not just out of her league: she knew that giving her body to a man who had no capacity for love would only end with her heart bleeding on the floor.

When the driver had taken them to the airport outside New York City and they'd boarded his jet, she'd waited a little breathlessly for his reaction. Would he punish her with the silent treatment? Give up his vow of fidelity and start texting some more accommodating woman? Or, worst fear of all, would he try to seduce her on the spacious white leather sofa of the jet's cabin, when she had nowhere to flee?

If so, she honestly didn't know how long she could hold out, not against him, not against her own treacherous, desperate desire.

Instead, Theo had done something she'd never expected. He'd neither punished her nor pressed his sensual advantage.

He'd acted like a friend.

Theo had been solicitous of Emmie's comfort, asking the flight attendant for food and drinks that he thought might tempt her. When he'd suggested that they change out of their wedding clothes into *something more comfortable*, she'd braced herself—until he'd come out of the back room of the jet's cabin wearing a faded rock-concert

T-shirt and slim-fitting sweatpants. He actually wanted her to be *comfortable*.

So a little nervously, she'd changed out of her wedding dress and high heels into comfy leggings and an oversize hoodie emblazoned with the name of her community college. They'd washed down hors d'oeuvres and a charcuterie platter with sparkling water and soda and watched a mutually agreed-upon movie. Nervous of rom-coms, she'd argued in favor of a female-led comedy, and he'd let her talk him into it. It was only later that she realized his negotiation had been only pretense. He'd let her choose.

Midway through the movie, sated and sleepy, she'd fallen asleep. She'd woken over the Atlantic to find Theo sleeping beside her on the white leather sofa, his arm protectively over her shoulders, his cheek resting on the top of her head.

They'd arrived at Lyra yesterday, coming by speedboat from the nearest airstrip at Paros, a few islands over. She'd closed her eyes, feeling the sun on her face and wind through her hair, then heard her husband's apologetic voice beside her.

"The yacht is stuck in Athens till tomorrow, I'm afraid. We'll have to manage at the local hotel tonight."

He'd looked so regretful, as if he really feared he was disappointing her, that Emmie expected to find Lyra an abandoned ghost village and the local hotel a dilapidated shepherd's hovel.

Instead, she'd discovered a charming Greek village clinging to the edge of the sea, full of kind, friendly people. Waking ten minutes ago, she'd felt refreshed, reborn, after a night of deep, delicious sleep as her husband had held her in his arms.

Held her. Just held her.

Maybe this marriage was going to work after all.

As long as their partnership was based only on comfort, support and friendship—

But as she looked back at the tiny double bed in the small room, her eyes forgot they were *friends…only friends…just friends* and unwillingly caressed the length of his powerful tanned body half-hidden beneath the tangle of sheets. The muscles of his chest stood out starkly, the morning sunlight gleaming over his thick biceps and thighs, hardened from his gym habit.

He was wearing only boxer shorts. She dimly recalled hearing him get up at sunrise, quietly change his clothes and go out. When he'd returned, he'd gone to the tiny en suite and turned on the shower. Gauging by the running shoes, T-shirt and shorts left on the floor, he must have gone for a run.

What drove him? she wondered. Why did he throw his body so hard at everything, whether it was working superhuman hours or going for a long run after very few hours of sleep?

Her gaze lingered on his hard-muscled chest, following the dark line of hair down his six-pack abs to the very center of his masculine body, beneath the boxer shorts mostly hidden by the cotton sheets twisted between his sprawled, powerful legs.

"Morning."

At Theo's deep, lazy voice, she looked up sharply, her cheeks hot. With his arm still tossed above his head on the pillow, he gave a wicked, amused smile. He'd clearly caught her perusing his near-naked body.

"Morning." She trembled a little, waiting for him to hold out his hand, to try to tempt her to join him in bed. Could she resist? Could she refuse?

Instead, he sat up in bed, smiling. "I'm starving. Want some breakfast?"

She smiled back, relieved. "Sure…"

Then her throat closed as he rose from the bed, giving her a full view of his powerful, nearly naked body. She saw the scarred flesh of his ankle, burned from an engine fire in a long-ago car race. She caught her breath as he bent over, giving her a view of his muscled back, the boxers straining over the powerful curve of his backside as he dug through his suitcase. Cheeks burning, she turned away, staring out the window at the sea.

"Ready." Dressed casually in a collared linen shirt and khaki shorts, he gave her an innocent smile, even as she thought she saw a glint of wicked amusement in his eyes. And his lips curved upward at the edges—

Oh, heaven. How had her gaze fallen to his lips? She swallowed. "Ready."

But her cheeks still felt hot as they went downstairs to share a late-morning breakfast on the taverna's small patio at the water's edge.

She had dressed modestly in the loose blue cotton sundress and sandals she'd bought in the village yesterday, her hair in a simple ponytail. With only sunscreen applied to her skin, she looked like a tourist and respectable married pregnant lady, she hoped, no different from any other… No one would know their honeymoon was chaste, she told herself. Biting her lip, she stared down at the huge rock on her left hand as the innkeeper spoke to Theo, beaming, clearly delighted to discover that his guest spoke fluent Greek.

Sipping her creamy decaf coffee, Emmie looked around at the other guests who'd straggled down to breakfast late. They all looked like honeymooners for sure, with a post-sex glow. One young couple, holding hands over the table, kept kissing each other when they thought no one was looking. Her heart twisted with unwelcome envy.

"I'm sorry this honeymoon is such a disappointment." She turned to her husband wide-eyed, suddenly terrified he'd read her mind. Sipping his own black coffee, he gave her a mild smile. "With the yacht coming late."

"I don't mind," she answered, relieved. "I like it here." At the rise of his skeptical black eyebrows, she added a little defensively, "Lyra is the most beautiful, charming, friendly place I've ever seen."

He glanced up as the innkeeper brought their breakfasts and departed. "If you say so."

Taking a bite of her flaky pastry—ah, heavenly butter!— Emmie closed her eyes in bliss, mumbling, "If you don't like Lyra, why did you bring us here on honeymoon?"

His eyes flickered. "Our honeymoon starts on the yacht." He stabbed his eggs with his fork. "Our stop in Lyra is just an unpleasant errand I need to finish first."

Lyra unpleasant? She nearly choked on her second pastry. Washing it down with sweet, creamy coffee, she wiped her mouth. "I'm happy here."

"No one is happy here," he muttered.

Did he know this island well? She frowned, trying to remember anything he might have told her about Greece when she was his secretary. But there was nothing. He'd never spoken about his past in Greece, ever. She asked bluntly, "What's your errand?"

Theo looked at her, his jaw tight. "You deserve the honeymoon of your dreams, Emmie. You'll have it. I promise you. You'll be cherished in luxury on my yacht, waited on by a ten-person staff. We'll visit Santorini, where a friend is hosting a party for us. It should be very glamorous. Then Mykonos."

"Glamorous," Emmie sighed.

His lips curved. "Didn't you notice the clothes in your suitcase?"

Emmie had, to her dismay. After they'd arrived in Greece, he'd presented her with a Louis Vuitton trunk graced with her new initials, E. S. K., filled with new designer clothes that fit her pregnant body perfectly, including cocktail dresses and resort wear—obviously arranged by a stylist, at great expense. It was still in lockup at the harbor, awaiting to be loaded onto the yacht.

But she'd seen a flash of prices on the tags. A two-thousand-dollar swimsuit cover-up from Prada? Seriously? Once they were back in New York, she vowed to take it straight back to the stylist for a refund. Even if her husband was crazy rich, that didn't mean their spending should be crazy stupid.

Especially not when, as she and Theo had wandered Lyra's narrow cobblestone village road yesterday afternoon, she'd found swimsuit cover-ups for just ten euros and cotton sundresses for twelve, one of which she was wearing now. She looked down at her hand, twisting her diamond ring nervously. "We could skip Mykonos and Santorini and just stay in Lyra."

"Thank you, but you don't need to pretend. This place is a hellhole." His jaw was tight as he looked up at the charming taverna hotel that she'd taken a million pictures of with her phone since yesterday. "I'm sorry. You deserve better."

Her brow furrowed. Hellhole?

Was he in some alternate reality?

In her time on this island, she'd felt nothing but joy. Emmie wasn't sure why. Was it because, for the first time in her life, she was on vacation? With no responsibilities, no family to cook and clean for, no number-crunching in a basement cubicle or billionaire-wrangling over business schedules?

She didn't have to serve anyone or rush anywhere. She'd just been able to do whatever she pleased. She'd wandered the village on a whim, exclaiming with delight over everything, from the sweet cat curled up on a sunny windowsill, to the children dragging a kite, to the housewife sweeping her doorway and the old man leading a herd of black-faced sheep down the cobblestones. Emmie was in heaven.

And she'd assumed Theo felt the same. But now, looking back, she realized he'd simply followed her, encouraging her happiness without taking part in it. If anything, Theo seemed to go out of his way to be a stranger in Lyra, never introducing himself, avoiding people's eyes, as if deliberately acting the part of the rich, arrogant American tourist.

The truth was, though he'd tried to hide it, he'd been tense since they'd arrived here. She should have realized it earlier, when she saw he'd gone for a long run at dawn. It was how he dealt with stress. Exercise—or sex. Which obviously he wasn't getting.

She swallowed. What was the mysterious errand? "Why don't you like Lyra?"

His jaw tightened again as he looked away. "It's unfortunate the yacht-engine repair took longer than expected. A part had to be flown in from Rotterdam. But we'll be sleeping onboard tonight, I assure you."

Emmie looked past the small fishing boats to the enormous, modern yacht approaching the harbor and felt strangely let down. "Is that it?"

"Yes. Finally." Theo hesitated. "As I told you, I have an errand to run later today. It'll take me a few hours…"

"I'll come."

"No." Then added more gently, "If you're truly enjoying

Lyra, I'm sure you'd prefer to spend your last hours shopping and relaxing, rather than dealing with some dreary errand."

"But what is it? Does it have to do with your new property in Greece? The one you mentioned at the wedding?"

Theo carefully ate a bite of dry toast then tossed the rest back on the plate. He gave her a smile that didn't meet his eyes. "You'll be all right for a few hours without me? You won't be lonely on your own?"

Of course she wouldn't be all right. What bride would appreciate being abandoned on the second day of her honeymoon, so the groom could disappear on a mysterious errand he refused to discuss?

But friendship went both ways. She wanted to be supportive, not clingy. So she forced herself to smile. "I'll be fine."

"Good." His handsome face held no expression as he tossed down his linen napkin. Looking at her downcast face, he relented. "But we have a few hours to enjoy ourselves first. What do you say we go to the beach?"

She brightened. "I'd love that."

Smiling, Theo tossed a pile of euros on the table, leaving an enormous tip. As they went upstairs to get changed, Emmie hummed a happy song to herself as they climbed the stairs, thrilled at the thought of spending time on the famous white sand beach of a bona fide Greek island.

"This is going to be so fun—" But as she turned back to her husband on the rickety stairs, his handsome face was twisted with so much grief and rage, she caught her breath.

The darkness in his expression was quickly masked as their eyes met. He smoothed his face into a smile. "I certainly hope so."

And Emmie couldn't help but wonder how it was possible that this quaint Greek island, which to her seemed so sunny and bright, was a hellhole that Theo couldn't wait to leave.

From the moment Theo saw the small rocky island of Lyra, he'd known bringing Emmie here was a mistake.

He'd brought the small, wrapped package from the safe of his Manhattan office to do what he'd been delayed from doing last week: watching from a distance as the charred ruin of his past was finally completely destroyed. Then he'd meant to drop the package into the sea, as Sofia had asked.

But there had been complications. The yacht's faulty engine leaving it docked in Athens. Sofia coming to Lyra after he'd specifically told her to stay in Paris. His wife starting to ask questions.

This wasn't how Theo had imagined his revenge would be.

Just climbing out of the speedboat onto the dock in Lyra's small harbor, returning to this place he'd sworn he'd never set foot on again, had caused a physical reaction. Even now, everywhere he looked made his skin crawl with memory, spiders and centipedes of repressed tragedy, little feet of horror whispering up and down his spine.

Walking through the tiny village which Emmie proclaimed *charming*, all he could see were the ghosts of the past. He'd seen her startled eyes when he'd called it a *hellhole*, and he'd known he'd revealed too much, been too honest about his feelings. But anytime he wasn't in her arms, focused on the long game of his slow seduction, he was on edge.

So far, no one had recognized him. He'd had a different surname then. He'd had so many names as a child. His father's. Then his mother's. He'd had three different stepfathers, none of whom had legally adopted him, but his mother always insisted on calling him by each new surname, as if that could bind her new husband to her son, to make them a family. Hopeless. Stupid.

Then it all ended in flames…

The torture of his own memories caused an overlay of pain over every pretty whitewashed building with blue shutters, an invisible shroud suffocating the rocky shoreline and clear blue water.

He'd been helpless as a boy. Helpless to save his family, even to save himself.

Until he finally had—at unbearable cost…

Theo couldn't relax. Since he'd arrived, he'd barely slept. So he'd gone for a run that morning, pushing himself hard, sprinting the eight-mile trail around the edge of the cliffs, hoping to outrun all his demons.

He ran past an old house and saw the gray-haired, wrinkled version of a woman he vaguely remembered. One who'd once called the police when she'd found him stumbling down the road as a boy, broken and covered in his own blood. Now, the old woman's eyes narrowed as he ran past.

But he didn't stop. He didn't want to be recognized as that boy. Not by anyone. Not even himself.

For decades, he'd seen the charred ruin in his dreams. Theo had bought the ruined property on Lyra because he'd hoped if he took possession of hell, it would loosen its jaws around his soul. But on his run, when he'd seen the burned debris in the distance, he'd stopped cold.

Theo had thought, returning to Lyra as a self-made billionaire with a wife and a child on the way, he'd prove his past was finally behind him, that he'd feel proud and strong, that he'd finally leave the helpless boy behind.

But one look at that scene and he'd realized nothing had changed inside him, not really. Maybe it never would...

"Can you believe it?" Emmie's joyful face looked up at him beneath the wide-brimmed sun hat she'd bought yesterday with *Lyra* stitched across the top in Greek letters. In spite of her stringent application of sunscreen, her legs and arms were already turning tan, with the slightest hint of pink, and he saw freckles on her upturned nose. "A secret beach!"

It took him a moment to brush away old ghosts and come back to the present. By then, Emmie had already dropped her cheap straw beach bag on the white sand. She yanked her white sleeveless cover-up off over her head, revealing a turquoise string bikini as she raced out into the blue water with a joyful whoop.

Standing alone on the beach, Theo stared out at her.

Her bikini caressed her pregnant curves as she kicked at the surf, spreading her arms wide and turning her face to the sun. The little triangle tops of the bra barely contained her overflowing breasts, and the bikini bottom, with strings tied in bows at her hips, was half-hidden by her belly.

Theo was hard just looking at her. But then, he felt like he'd been hard from the moment of their marriage. Repressing his desire, treating her with asexual kindness and concern, cuddling with her while they watched that awful comedy on the jet—and most difficult of all, having her sleep next to him in bed, for the love of heaven, feeling her soft, sensual body move against his groin as she sighed and moaned in sleep—

Remembering, he breathed a strangled curse. A man could only endure so much. He didn't know how much longer he could bear it.

When would his wife finally give in to her own desire and make the first move? When?

It amazed him now that he'd thought her plain before he hired her. How had Emmie contrived to camouflage her incredible beauty for months at the office, in the unflattering suits and tightly prim hairstyles of the efficient, sexless secretary, before he'd finally, truly seen her?

Now, Theo stared at her as she waded into the blue water like Aphrodite, golden beneath the sun. Emmie Swenson Katrakis was the most beautiful woman he'd ever known.

More than beautiful: she was magic. She was the only one who could make him forget. The only one who could chase the ghosts away. Making love to her was all he could think about.

Which meant she was his addiction. Right or wrong, he had to keep her close. So he could keep touching her, looking at her. And when she surrendered to temptation and took him back into her bed, he'd finally feel peace, in the explosion of euphoria as he took her…again and again…

"What are you waiting for?" she called, swimming and kicking in the sea. "Come join me!"

Emmie was chest-deep, the surface of the water clinging to her swollen breasts, sliding slowly over her skin and the tiny clinging fabric. The shock between cool water and warm air caused her nipples to pebble beneath the material. He could see the shape of them, even from here.

He needed no further invitation. He ripped off his shirt and tossed his phone down on top of it. Wearing only his blue swim trunks, he plunged into the water, letting the sea wash him clean before he resurfaced beside her. Pulling her into his arms, he kissed her in the Greek sun, just for a split second, as salty water splashed over them both.

With a laugh, she pulled away and ducked her body

back beneath the water. Playfully, she kicked a wave of water over him.

With a low growl, he threw himself in pursuit of her, and with a mock scream she swam away. They played together in the water on the private, deserted beach, and he somehow laughed harder than he had in a long time.

Finally, as the sun started to lower in the sky, he remembered the errand and felt a shadow over his soul. They waded back to the sandy beach. He checked the time and told himself he could take a few more moments, just a few. He spread their blanket beneath the scrawny shade of a single olive tree, clinging to the edge of some rocks.

He dried her off with a towel and froze, looking down at her, his heart pounding. He thought of stretching her out on the sun-warmed blanket and taking her right there on the white sand. But shepherds had sometimes wandered through here following their charges, and even when he was younger there had been an occasional backpacker who heard about the secret beach. But maybe—

"How did you even know about this place?" Emmie asked, yawning as she stretched her limbs out in the sun. "When I asked the innkeeper about a beach, she only told me about one up north. She called it the *tourist beach*."

"This one is kept quiet. For locals."

Her dark eyelashes fluttered open as she peeked at him. "Then, how did you know about it?"

Theo felt the low rumble of tension go through his body, like dark clouds on the edge of his consciousness, crackling the air with threat of a coming storm.

No, he thought. Please. He didn't want to think about it. Let him enjoy this just a little longer. Just an hour. A few more minutes.

"Theo." He felt her small hand reach up to cup his rough, unshaven chin. "What is it? What won't you tell me?"

For a moment, he closed his eyes, holding his breath. Her touch lured him—tempted him unbearably. All he wanted to do was pull her close, to kiss her, to feel her naked body against his own, to plunge into her, to lose his mind in the sweet madness between them.

And yet he forced himself to turn away. "It doesn't matter—"

But Emmie held onto his shoulders. Their eyes locked.

Lifting her head, she hesitated for the space of a breath. Then she kissed him. A brief brush of her lips against his.

Then she drew back, her violet eyes luminous in the Greek sun.

With an intake of breath, he pulled her into his arms, on the soft blanket and kissed her hungrily.

Their lips met like fire, and she clung to him—he clung to her—it was everything he'd waited for and more…

Pulling away with a gasp, he kissed down her neck, his hands roaming over her warm, bare skin—her breasts, her belly, her hips. He reached for the tie of her bikini top at the nape of her neck. His fingers fumbled with the effort, as if he were an untried boy—

Nearby, his phone rang. Squeezing his eyes shut, he tried to ignore the sound. But it kept ringing and ringing until finally, with a curse, he snatched it off the blanket, half-intending to toss it into the sea.

Then he saw the number of the person calling. It was like a splash of cold water in his face. Glancing at Emmie, he stood up unsteadily, putting the phone to his ear, walking away from the blanket beneath the olive tree. He spoke quietly into the phone, in Greek, praying his voice sounded calm, praying his wife wouldn't listen, wouldn't care, wouldn't ask questions.

Speaking quickly, he finished the call as soon as possible. But when he turned back, Emmie was sitting up, staring at him, her face pale beneath her freckles.

"Who's Sofia?" she demanded.

CHAPTER SEVEN

THREE EMOTIONS WENT through Emmie at the phone call, in a chain reaction.

The first was anger. She hated the person calling, whoever it might be. And she was none too pleased at her husband for answering his phone, either.

Then anger was washed away by relief as she realized what she'd nearly let happen: a total collapse of her willpower. Theo had been caressing her hair, both of them still wet from splashing in the surf, his dark eyes smiling down at her, beneath the bluffs and shade of the olive tree. She'd kissed him almost without thinking.

If not for the interruption of the phone call, they might have made love right then and there on the beach, beneath the eyes of any random shepherd passing by on the bluffs above. Really, she should be grateful to the unknown caller for preventing that disaster.

But as her husband paced the beach with his phone, speaking low in Greek, Emmie didn't feel exactly grateful. Her gaze slid over the tanned muscles of his bare back, the hard curve of his backside in the swim trunks, down his powerful thighs and calves, laced with dark hair as she watched him walk back and forth with his bare feet on the white sand.

Her husband's tone was increasingly tense, as if he were trying to convince the caller of something. Then she heard him clearly say a name amid all his impenetrable Greek. A woman's name. Sofia.

And Emmie felt a brand-new emotion. The strongest of all.

Fear.

Theo hadn't walked away with his phone to be polite, she realized; he didn't want her to know what he was talking about.

Or to whom.

"Who's Sofia?" she'd blurted out as he'd turned to face her. And his expression turned dark.

"You were listening? To my private phone call?"

"I—I didn't mean to," she stammered. Her cheeks went hot. "I couldn't help but overhear."

"Couldn't help but intrude? Even though I walked away from you and spoke in a language I know you don't understand? You still make these accusations!"

"Accusations?" she gasped. What accusations?

"It's late." Scowling, he reached for his shirt, then the bag. "I'll take you back to the hotel."

She felt somehow embarrassed, ashamed, as if she'd been rude and nosy, as if she were the one to blame for the sudden chill between them. She tried to keep up with her husband's long stride, carrying the sagging blanket in her arms as they hurried up the long, winding road back to the village. But how was it her fault? He was clearly keeping secrets from her—and not very well. With so many dark hints, it was almost as if he were goading her to ask questions!

Whatever the reason, Emmie didn't like to be at odds.

As they reached the tiny hotel room, she turned to him and said quietly, "Maybe we should talk."

"No time." Yanking off his beach clothes, he didn't even bother to hide his naked body from her as he pulled on a sleek long-sleeved black shirt and tailored black trousers. "I'm already running late. I'll be back in a few hours. Pack your things. I'll escort you to the yacht when I return."

"Okay," she said falteringly. "Have a good—"

But he'd already left, the door slamming closed behind him.

Emmie showered alone in the tiny en suite. When she came out into the bedroom, wrapped in a white towel, the tiny bedroom, which had previously seemed so cozy and tight, seemed cavernous in its emptiness.

Where had Theo gone? What was his errand?

Who was Sofia?

All her earlier happiness had evaporated like mist in sun. Slowly, she pulled on cotton panties and bra and a floral sundress she'd bought at the tourist shop in the village. Brushing her long damp hair, she pulled it back in a ponytail. In the small mirror, she noticed her skin had a healthy glow from the sun.

Or maybe it was from her sudden surge of rage.

How dare Theo treat her like this? Emmie was not his secretary anymore, paid to serve his interests, at his pleasure. She was his wife. She deserved to know these secrets he kept hinting at!

Setting her jaw, she pulled on sandals, grabbed her straw bag and stomped out of the hotel room to look for him.

Ten minutes later, her anger had turned to despair. She would not find him—of course she wouldn't, not if he didn't want her to. It was so unfair. How could Theo make her so miserable, even though she wasn't even sleeping with him?

What was the point of denying them both the pleasure, if she was just going to end up miserable anyway?

Walking up the cobblestoned street, she felt a lump in her throat. She put on cheap sunglasses from her bag to hide the tears in her eyes.

Her lips parted when she saw a tall, broad-shouldered man, in a black shirt and trousers which seemed much too formal for the island, walking down a narrow alley with a pretty young black-haired woman. They walked side by side, not touching, but something about the way they spoke quietly insinuated a certain…intimacy.

Emmie ducked back behind a corner, then peeked around it, watching as they continued down the hill toward the marina. Furtively, a little guiltily, she followed the couple down the paths to the docks.

Theo and the unknown girl—Sofia?—walked down the largest wooden dock toward a vintage wooden speedboat waiting with a uniformed crew member at the steering wheel. Farther out in the harbor, Emmie saw her husband's gleaming, modern yacht, named *Future 2*, replacing Theo's starter yacht *Future* of a decade before. She'd never been on either yacht as his secretary.

Emmie watched as he helped the girl climb into the waiting speedboat. On impulse, she bolted toward the marina.

"No!" she cried, running down the wooden dock. "Wait!"

Theo stared back at her with shock. Turning, he spoke in a low voice to the black-haired girl, who shrugged.

As Emmie reached the end, she threw herself into the small speedboat, still panting from her sprint. Theo caught her as she fell. Setting her aright, he glared at her, then let her go, folding his arms.

"I gave you specific instructions. To remain at the hotel."

"I'm not your secretary. You can't give me orders." Emmie's cheeks burned as she turned to the pretty brunette. Sticking out her hand, she said politely, "Hi, I'm Emmie. I assume you're Sofia?"

The girl glanced briefly at Theo, then said, "Yes?"

Was that a question or answer? Emmie couldn't tell if she even understood English. As they shook hands, the brunette raised her eyebrow at Theo, who gave a small, disgusted shake of his head.

"Go," he ordered the boat's driver. The crewman pressed on the gas, whirling the speedboat from the docks toward the yacht in the bay. Other than the loud engine, there was silence. No one tried to explain anything to Emmie.

"So." Emmie licked her lips, feeling awkward and foolish. "What's this all about?"

The girl just looked out at the water.

"Français?" Emmie tried hopefully in her schoolgirl French. Still nothing. And the only Greek word she knew was *efaristo*, which seemed highly inappropriate for her current feelings.

"Since you insisted on coming," Theo told Emmie coldly, "sit down and try not to be a nuisance."

Nuisance? Sitting abruptly in a cushioned seat, Emmie ground her teeth as she looked back at the vanishing shoreline and charming village clinging to the rocks. She'd give *him* nuisance.

The speedboat soon arrived at the enormous yacht, and they were assisted up the steps by uniformed crew, then kicked off their shoes, as apparently everyone went in socks and bare feet on yachts. Not as glamorous as she'd imagined, Emmie thought, surveying her own chipped toenail polish dourly.

They reached the wide deck, with its comfortable chairs and views in every direction. As the yacht started to move, a different member of the crew pushed a flute of champagne into Theo's hand, then the girl's, then even Emmie's.

She looked at the crystal flute, bewildered. Why would anyone give a pregnant woman champagne? In fact, it seemed strange that Theo and the dark-haired girl had champagne, too. Neither seemed to be celebrating.

If anything, her husband looked haunted, his dark eyes shadowed as he kept glancing down at the waiflike brunette. The girl just gripped the yacht's railing and stared out at the sea, her expression pitiable.

Emmie didn't understand any of this.

Holding her untasted flute, Emmie went inside the sliding glass door and handed it to a member of the crew in a white short-sleeved shirt and shorts. "Here, thank you very much, but I don't need this."

"Of course, ma'am." Taking it readily, he touched his cap respectfully and turned away. She stopped him.

"Excuse me, but...um...where are we going?"

The young man looked confused. "To the other side of the island, ma'am. For the best view."

"Ah. Yes. Of course. Thank you," she said, nodding sagely, as she'd sometimes seen her father and brothers do when they had no idea what someone was talking about. Going back out on the open deck, she hugged herself in the warm Greek wind as the yacht sliced through the ocean waves. She looked across the deck toward Theo and the girl.

She couldn't imagine him taking a mistress, not after just two days of marriage, and parading her in front of Emmie! No, surely not. There had to be some other explanation for why he'd come to Lyra, a place he clearly hated, to go on a yachting excursion in secret. With a pretty brunette.

Didn't there?

It didn't take long for them to reach the other side of the

island. From this side, the shore was rocky, brown, bare of trees, far from civilization. Her eyes widened when she saw the burned-out ruin of a building clinging alone to the side. A grand old house, long since destroyed.

Going to Theo, she whispered, "What is that?"

His dark eyes brooded as he stared back at the island, gripping the railing. He said flatly, "A house."

"I can see that." Staring at the shell, she thought of Daphne du Maurier's tragic burned Manderley. "But whose?"

Turning to her, he bit out coldly, "Mine."

"Oh," Emmie said, confused. There was nothing left but the mansion's blackened bones, faded by sun, in ruins for years or even decades. Then she noticed men in hard hats, small from this distance, waiting beside the ruin, a small battalion with heavy machinery, excavators, loaders, bulldozers. She frowned, trying to make sense of it. She said faintly, "You're here to rebuild?"

"No. To destroy." Looking out at the site with grim satisfaction, Theo gestured to the captain, who spoke quietly into a phone. He turned back to Emmie with cold black eyes. "And to answer your question, Sofia is my sister."

Theo watched across the water as men in hard hats, having received the go-ahead, plowed forward with two excavators and a bulldozer, knocking down the last charred walls of the dilapidated house.

Nearby, he heard a choked sniffle. Sofia was gripping the railing, her dark eyes filled with anguish as she looked out at their former home in the twilight.

Without a word, he went to stand beside her. Unsure how to offer comfort, he put his arm around her uncertainly. She leaned against him, silently weeping, never looking away from the island, as the last vestiges of their childhood home were flattened and wiped off the face of the earth.

Looking down, Theo dimly saw a flute in his hand. He'd ordered the very best champagne from his cellar specifically for the occasion. But when he'd pictured this day, destroying the property now that it was his at last, he'd thought he'd feel a sense of joy, triumph—or at least relief.

Instead Theo felt sick, his insides churning. Glancing behind him on the deck, he saw Emmie watching him. He felt her gaze. Her *silence*. She'd been startled when he'd said Sofia was his sister, but she hadn't asked any questions. Now, he was suddenly afraid it was because she didn't need to. More than anyone else, she'd always had a knack for seeing past his defenses, even as his secretary.

And now…

His throat tightened.

Cold. Cold. He had to be cold. To show emotion was weakness. A man had to be strong, or both he and the people he loved would suffer. He had to be ice.

"Cheers," Theo forced himself to say in English, holding up his flute. Sofia stared at him with black tearstained eyes, then finally lifted her own. He clinked his glass against hers, and they each managed a sip of champagne. Reaching into his pocket, he handed her the small brown paper-wrapped package he'd taken from his office safe.

Setting her glass down on a nearby table, she looked at the small package. She said in Greek, "Is it…?"

"Naí." Yes.

Unwrapping it, she pulled out a small gold locket. Clutching it tightly in her hand, she shuddered. "Thank you," she said in a whisper, then took a deep breath. "But…"

"But?"

She looked back at the ruin. "I want to be there."

Theo swallowed. His voice was harsher than he intended as he said, "We're close enough."

"I want the dirt beneath my feet."

"No," he said helplessly, but even as he said it, he knew he would do it. After everything he'd done—and everything he *hadn't* done—he owed her anything she wanted, and more.

Setting his jaw, Theo turned to the captain and spoke a few quiet words. After conferring into his phone, the man replied in the same language.

Theo returned to his sister. "The site's not safe. They still need to fill in the foundation and pull any remaining materials."

She simply lifted her eyes to his, waiting.

Theo sighed. He'd tried to talk Sofia out of coming here today. His original plan had been to film the house's destruction, then send the video to her in Paris. He'd been delayed by his rush back to stop Emmie's wedding in New York. Then Sofia had informed him she'd flown in from Paris to be on the island when the demolition happened.

So he'd revised the plan. He and his bride would sail past Lyra on the yacht, as if by chance, right as the house was demolished. He'd let Emmie believe he was filming the demolition of an interesting ruin, nothing more, then he'd send the video to Sofia at the tiny, unused cottage in the village that she'd inherited from her adoptive family.

But the one-day delay caused by the yacht's needed repair had ended that plan, too. He'd known from the moment he stepped onto Lyra that he didn't want Emmie with him when the house was razed. Having to act casual, to show no emotion, to hide his feelings from her would have been difficult. So he'd decided to leave her at the hotel and go alone on his yacht to film the event from a distance.

Then Sofia had called that afternoon to say she'd changed her mind. She was determined to come with him today and see the teardown in person, and no amount of his arguing had persuaded her otherwise.

First Sofia, now Emmie. Why did the two women he cared about the most insist on fighting his efforts to protect them from pain? Their pain—and his?

Theo looked down at his dark-haired sister. When he'd knocked on her door that afternoon, it had been the first time he'd seen her in person since she was five. He'd had to blink hard to hide the sting in his eyes as he'd hugged her. In some ways, she would always be that child to him. A child who'd deserved a better brother than Theo. And still did.

Now, Sofia set her jaw. "I don't care about *safe*. I need this, Theo." Her gaze wandered back to the ruin on the hill. "Otherwise, part of me will always be trapped there."

He glanced back at Emmie, still standing alone at the railing a few feet away, pretending she wasn't interested in their discussion, pretending she wasn't offended that they continued to speak Greek in front of her. Theo and Sofia could have easily spoken English; his sister spoke the language well, along with French and German and Spanish. He'd paid for her to attend good schools across Europe.

It was a miracle some enterprising journalist hadn't discovered Theo's whole sordid childhood. The confusion of his five different surnames as a boy had probably helped. It was only after his uncle had brought him to America at sixteen that he'd used his long-dead father's surname of Katrakis.

The name Theo had at fifteen, when his mother and stepfather died, had been Papadopolous. His stepfather's name. It had also been Sofia's surname before she was adopted. The neighbor had adopted only Sofia, not Theo.

Who wouldn't want a sweet little orphan girl? Who would ever want a hardened, violent, grief-stricken teenage boy?

His heart was pounding strangely. He felt beads of sweat on his forehead in spite of the cooling breeze. He glanced sideways at Emmie. She was staring down over the slanted sunlight into the dark water below, her shoulders tight beneath the thin straps of her floral sundress.

How he wished she'd just stayed at the hotel. He would have retrieved her after this was all over and done with, and they'd have sailed off into the sunset. She wouldn't have known about Sofia or the house, he'd have had nothing to evade, and they both would have been happier.

"Well, Theo?" Sofia asked in Greek. "Can we?"

"Fine," he said heavily. His belly roiled at the thought of setting foot there. But as he looked at his little sister's pale, haunted face, he knew any pain would be worth it to give her the slightest bit of peace.

As he and Sofia left, he saw the question in Emmie's eyes and answered it with a shake of his head. He didn't want her to accompany them. Because he couldn't tell her the truth about their past, his and Sofia's. And he didn't want to lie to her.

After putting on their shoes, he led Sofia down the steep steps into the small speedboat.

Looking up, Theo had one last glance of Emmie watching from the top deck, the lowering red and orange sun shining through her hair like gold, her expression darkened by shadow. Then the boat took them swiftly—far too swiftly—to shore.

The old dock was long gone, so they had to hop out and wade through knee-deep water. He offered to carry Sofia, but she shook her head. They stumbled onto the beach he'd once paced as a desperate teenager, scared out of his mind.

Theo stopped and looked back at the sun setting over the horizon. Except for the silhouette of the yacht, the view was the same now that it had been then. If he closed his eyes, he could still feel the same panic, the frantic beat of his heart.

Theo was relieved when Sofia called to him, breaking the spell. Together, they trudged the overgrown path up the dry, rocky hill, sea water sluicing off their bare legs and squishing in their shoes.

The big house had been scraped away. When they reached the edge of the site, he stopped to speak to one of the hired demolishers.

His sister staggered forward. Falling to her knees, she touched the dry earth where her bedroom had been, then covered her face with a sob. Theo watched, his shoulders taut, his eyes dry. Digging a hole with her hands, Sofia she took the small gold locket from her pocket and dropped it in. She filled in the hole, smoothing dirt over it. Then she looked down at the cracked stone walls of the old basement on the other side of the structure, half-destroyed and filled with debris, little more than a hole in the ground.

"Tell them to yank it out," she said in a low voice. "Every single stone."

The sun was dying, bleeding red across the sea, by the time they returned to the yacht. Theo's steps were heavy as Sofia fled to the cushioned seats on deck, to sit alone in shadows with her grief. Emmie was nowhere to be seen.

"Where is my wife?" he asked.

"I believe she was fatigued after dinner," the captain replied, "and went to rest in your quarters, sir."

Theo was glad he didn't have to worry about hiding his feelings from her. Being strong in the face of Sofia's grief and pain was difficult enough. He went to sit by his sister, holding her as she cried.

The yacht swiftly returned to the village harbor. Once they were at anchor, he and Sofia took a speedboat to the dock. Sending staffers back to the taverna hotel to pay his bill and collect his and Emmie's things, Theo walked Sofia to her little stone house on the edge of town, a summer cottage now rarely used by her adoptive family. When he left her at her door, she gave him a trembling smile, her eyes luminous.

"Thank you, Theo," she said and hugged him. "I'll be… better now."

Feeling a lump in his throat, he hugged her back. His voice was hoarse as he pulled away. "You deserve every happiness, Sofia." He hesitated. "If I can ever do anything for you, anything at all… Money, help, a quiet word in the right ear…"

Wiping her eyes, she whispered, "Just having you back in my life is all I ever wanted."

With a jerky nod, he turned away. But as Theo returned to the yacht, where his beautiful bride and glamorous honeymoon waited, Theo did not feel better. His muscles ached. His throat hurt. His soul felt sore.

He knew, even if Sofia did not, that his sister was better-off without him in her life. Today surely proved that. He thought of how Sofia had wept, her knees in the dirt, and closed his eyes, sick at heart. However much she might wish otherwise, she'd never forget he was the one to blame.

Reaching the yacht, he stood at the railing, watching as the pearlescent moon rose softly over the Aegean. He thought of drinking whiskey, or maybe guzzling the barely touched Dom Pérignon. He thought of burying himself in work, prepping for his upcoming pitch, the latest iteration of his dream project in Paris he'd pursued for years. None of it appealed.

Only one thing could save him.

Going through the yacht's sliding glass doors, he went down the hall to his private suite. In the darkness, he found his wife sleeping in the large bed.

He woke her with a kiss.

"Theo," she murmured. "What—"

His hand moved to her breast beneath her white sleeveless nightgown, as her lips parted, gasping against his. He deepened the kiss, pressing her back against the bed. He was desperate to touch her, to taste her skin. She wrenched away.

"Stop."

Startled, he stared at her in the slender dagger of moonlight pooling on the bed. She took a deep breath.

"Tell me," she said quietly. "About today."

Theo stiffened. It wasn't enough that Sofia knew his failures. Now Emmie wanted some rope to hang him with as well? "It's in the past. It doesn't matter."

She looked up at him. *Saw right through him.*

"What am I to you? Just the mother of your child? An accessory on your arm that you put in a box when you're done?"

He glared at her. "You know you're more."

"Do I?" She looked down at her hands, interlaced tightly over the blanket. "I want our marriage to work. But how can I feel like your partner, or even your friend, when you don't tell me anything?"

Theo set his jaw. "I don't want to talk about the past. Ever. It's not a happy story. Forget it. As I have—"

But as he moved toward her again, intending to kiss her into submission, she stopped him with a small hand pressed firmly to his chest. Her eyes pierced his. "Either explain, or get out."

Theo stared at her, his heart pounding. Snatching up a pillow, he rose from the bed. He turned to leave.

Then he stopped, staring blankly at the open door.

Emmie was his wife. If he kept her in the dark, yes, he'd remain safely in control. She couldn't despise him for his past or use it against him.

But what would it mean for their marriage? Now that she knew he was hiding something awful, how long would it be before any chance of intimacy between them—physical or otherwise—was utterly destroyed?

Theo turned back to face her. "Fine," he said hoarsely. "Don't say I didn't warn you."

CHAPTER EIGHT

AFTER A FRUSTRATING night when she'd tossed and turned, trying to understand the incomprehensible events yesterday, Emmie stared at her husband, scared to breathe, scared to break the spell. Was he finally, actually going to reveal his secrets?

Theo's jawline, dark and unshaven, clenched as he looked toward the open porthole, out at the moon-swept sea. Outside, she heard the plaintive call of seagulls.

"The ruin was once my home," he said softly. "Mine and Sofia's."

"In a mansion? On Lyra?" Her lips parted. "I thought you were found by your uncle, roaming the streets of Athens."

"I was—later." His lips curled humorlessly. "It's only because I had so many names as a boy that no one's ever learned the full story. Technically Sofia is my half sister. I was ten when she was born."

"She lives on Lyra?"

He exhaled.

"Paris," he said finally.

Honestly, it was like getting blood out of a turnip.

Clasping her hands in her lap over the king-size comforter, Emmie tried to control her desire to know more. She thought of the emotion she'd seen yesterday as Theo and his sister had watched the destruction on shore. To the untrained eye, he might have seemed stoic, but she'd seen his jaw tighten, his hands clench, his dark eyes blink hard and fast. Someone who didn't know him well might have thought he was angry.

But she'd seen Theo angry. Many times. He'd even been angry at her once or twice, when she'd been distracted by her mother's latest cancer prognosis and accidentally double-booked an appointment, then put a call through from an ex-mistress he was trying to avoid.

But what Emmie had seen in him yesterday went far beyond anger. There'd been an undercurrent of something powerful. Something he hadn't known how to deal with. She'd watched his tender concern for his young sister, who'd seemed devastated. And Emmie had known, whatever this dark cloud was over the siblings, it was so awful it had changed the course of their lives.

Very gently, she asked now, "What happened?"

Sitting abruptly on the bed beside her, Theo searched her gaze, and for a moment she thought he wouldn't answer. Then he said in a low voice, "I'll tell you. Then you'll never ask me about it again. Ever."

"All right."

"You know my father died when I was a baby." Theo looked down, twisting the plain gold band on his left hand. "My mother was an addict. Not just drugs. She was addicted to falling in love. She made…bad choices. My stepfather was the worst. He was handsome, rich. After two divorces, when she met him she thought she finally had the fairy tale. I was ten when we went to live on Lyra. But his money didn't last. He started blaming her. Hurting her. Then he hurt me when I tried to get between them. Then finally..." His throat seemed to close. He said hoarsely, "There was a fire. I was only able to save my sister."

"Oh, Theo," she whispered, reaching out to touch his arm. He didn't seem to notice.

"My mother always thought love would save her," he whispered. "It only brought her grief. And in the end... she died from it."

Emmie saw the tightness in his black eyes, heard the faint wildness of his breath in the shadowy bedroom of the yacht.

"I finally was able to take possession of the house. What was left of it. And Sofia and I needed to see the final demolition. To remember." His lips twisted. "Or maybe to forget."

She could feel the violence of repressed emotion radiating from him in waves. Theo looked up, his handsome face stark.

"Is there anything more you want to know?"

Emmie's heart was pounding. Did she need to know more? Did she even *want* to?

"Theo—"

Then she felt a hard kick beneath her ribs and sucked in her breath. She felt the kick again, and her lips lifted. Every time it happened, she felt the same sense of wonder. "Our baby's kicking."

He frowned. "Now?"

Pushing the covers away, she grabbed his hand and pressed it to her belly over her nightgown. "Feel it?"

His dark eyes widened, and then his jaw fell as he looked down at her. "That's our baby?"

She smiled. "That's him."

"Is that normal? I mean," Theo hesitated, "does it hurt? Do I need to call a doctor? Should I—"

"I'm fine," she said, laughing. "And yes, it's normal. I'm glad you felt it. I want you to be part of everything. Part of our lives."

Their eyes locked, with her hand resting over his larger one, entwined over her baby bump. Emmie's heart twisted. She suddenly realized what courage it must have taken for this intensely private man to tell her so much. She caressed his rough cheek.

"Thank you for telling me. I'm so sorry about what happened." She paused. "But I'll protect you now. For the rest of our lives."

Theo looked down at her in the bedroom filled with shadows. His dark eyes flickered, and the air between them suddenly crackled with electricity.

Cupping her face, he leaned forward and kissed her. No brief, timid peck, but a deep kiss full of yearning. Full of emotion and need.

Beneath her cotton nightgown, her breasts turned heavy, nipples tightening, as desire coiled low and deep inside her. She kissed him back hungrily, clinging to him across the bed.

She felt him shudder. His lips were hard on hers, ravenous, as if he'd been starving and she alone could save him. Then he wrenched back, his eyes gleaming, his voice low.

"Are you sure?"

In answer, she kissed him, pulling him back against her body, her fingertips gripping into his shoulders.

With a repressed gasp, he pushed her back into the pool of moonlight on the bed. As they kissed, they held each other tight, gasping for breath. Suddenly, they were tearing at each other's clothes. His shirt disappeared, then her nightgown, then the rest.

She wanted this. She was no longer afraid. Now she

knew that, caring for him as she did, she was going to suffer anyway. Why deny herself what she wanted most? Why
deny them both? Avoiding pleasure would not avoid pain.

As he stroked and kissed every inch of her, Emmie held
her breath, trembling with need. Her body was taut, aching. She gripped him closer, wanting more, *more*, to feel
him inside her, to finally possess him and make him her
own. He was the man she'd always wanted. And now he
was her husband. Hers forever.

Theo had never needed anyone like this.

He'd never felt so close to her. To anyone.

The shock of emotional intimacy, of being seen and
accepted by the woman he respected most, had cracked
through Theo's frozen soul. He'd taken the leap to reveal
part of his history to her, and she hadn't let him fall. Holding her naked body against his now was so utterly sweet
it was almost unbearable. He'd thought he wanted her before. That had been nothing, a grain of sand in a beach,
compared to the way he wanted her now.

As the dark Aegean swayed beneath the yacht, it took
every inch of Theo's self-control not to take her hard, now,
now, now.

But she was pregnant. He had to be gentle, even if the
effort cost him everything he had.

Taking a deep breath, he spread her body across the soft
blankets of the bed. Lowering his head, he savored each
rosy nipple, cupping her breasts, pale in the moonlight.
Until she started to sway beneath him like the waves.

He moved past the mound of her belly, gently stroking
her there, placing himself between her legs, parting her
thighs with his hands. He felt her shiver and shake as he
tasted her, until she gasped for breath, gripping the blan-

kets beneath her to steady herself. She cried out her release into the dark shadows of the bedroom, echoing inside the yacht, beneath the opalescent moonlight, along the ancient Greek sea.

Then, and only then, did he allow himself to slowly push inside her. Before, he'd wanted to take her hard and deep to chase his demons away.

Now he felt…different.

I'll protect you now. For the rest of our lives.

Emmie was his woman. His pregnant wife. It was his job to protect her and take care of her.

He felt a sudden flicker of fear. He'd already failed at protecting those he loved. People had died because of him.

Theo pushed the thought away desperately. This time would be different. He would make sure Emmie was always safe and cherished—

Lying down beside her on the big bed, he reached for her, lifting her over his body. Her weight was nothing, even though she was pregnant, but his hands shook with the effort it took for him to maintain his self-control as he slowly lowered her over him, her thighs spread to straddle his hips.

She gasped as she felt him push inside her, inch by hard inch, until finally she was pressed to the hilt, stretching her deep. For a moment, he held tight to her hips, not letting her move, as he exhaled, his body tight.

Then, slowly, she began to move, tentatively at first, then riding him harder and faster. His eyes opened, and he looked up at her, seeing her beautiful face with her eyes closed in bliss, her breasts swaying over her belly, her body tight. She tensed again, gripping his shoulders, and he heard her cry out even louder than she had before—

And he lost it. He exploded in ecstasy that he'd never

known, in pleasure he'd never imagined even possible. He heard a moan rise to a shout and realized it was his own.

She collapsed over him, sweaty and spent. Exhausted, still dazed by euphoria, he stroked her back. For a few sweet moments he just held her. He felt sated. Safe. Cherished.

For those few sweet moments, he felt like he deserved to still be alive.

The morning sea air was fresh against Emmie's skin as she sat alone at the deck's breakfast table. She touched her lips, still bruised from her husband's hungry kisses.

"Will there be anything else, Mrs. Katrakis?" a young, uniformed crewman asked respectfully, tucking his tray under his arm.

"No, thank you." As he departed, Emmie sipped sweet, creamy decaf coffee and took another bite of *bougatsa*, a buttery, flaky pastry, crunchy and sprinkled with powdered sugar on top, filled with sweet custard. She'd had two big pieces already, along with eggs and fruit.

She smoothed the napkin over her baby bump beneath her simple white shift dress. Brushing her long hair back from her shoulders, she sat back, looking out at the crystal blue sea. She should feel exhausted, with the way she'd spent the last two nights. But she didn't. Sleeping was wonderful, but not half so glorious as being awake with Theo.

They'd been docked here for two days now, just outside Santorini, and she'd never been so happy. Santorini, she thought. Another name for *heaven*.

"Good morning." Her husband fell into the chair across the small table with a wicked smile.

Golden sunlight poured over his high cheekbones and freshly shaven jaw. His open shirt revealed his powerful chest, tanned and caressed by light, shadows etching his muscled pecs and the taut six-pack. Emmie's eyes fell to the line of dark hair tracing down his belly before disappearing beneath the waistband of his swimming trunks.

Theo was handsome as sin. As always. They must have made love a dozen times since they'd left Lyra. How could she still want more? Mouth dry, she managed, "Going swimming this morning?"

"I was thinking about it." He poured steaming hot black coffee from a silver pot into a china cup edged with twenty-four-karat gold. "Care to join me?"

"I'm fine on the deck, thank you," she said, a little primly.

Leaning back in his chair, he smiled at her, his eyes glowing as he placed the edge of the china cup to his mouth. Right against his sensual lower lip.

"Stop that."

"Stop what?" he said innocently and took a sip, as if he hadn't been teasing her, making her imagine other places his mouth had recently been. She flushed, feeling her cheeks burn. He gave a sudden grin. "You're blushing."

"I'm not. You are," she said, a little incoherently. Coughing to cover, she looked out at the blue waves and the island of Santorini in the distance.

Theo stared at her silently, then reached for her hand. "What do you say, Mrs. Katrakis," he said softly. "Would you like to—"

He pulled his hand away as the member of the crew came back out on the deck through the sliding glass doors, holding a covered silver tray. He served Theo his plate of breakfast and departed. Emmie looked at his plate. Just eggs, meat and fruit.

She looked down at her own plate, empty except for the

scattering of crumbs. No buttery flaky pastries for him. That was Theo, she thought. No softness, no weakness.

Though he did have a few exceptions. He'd eat a whole loaf of bread, but only from a specific boulangerie in the sixth arrondissement in Paris. He'd devour a bowl of noodles big enough to feed a family of four from his favorite Tokyo shop.

Could she be as uniquely special, as desirable, to him as those hot, crusty baguettes? As that counter-service *yakisoba* from the Ginza district?

If so she'd have his adoration forever.

"What's so funny?" he said suspiciously.

She realized she'd been chuckling to herself—wishing she could be as special as a loaf of bread or stir-fried noodles! Stifling her laugh, she cleared her throat. "Nothing."

Tilting his head, he ate another bite of eggs. "Did I tell you we're invited to a party tonight?"

"That's tonight?"

"Not just a party. A wedding reception in our honor."

She was shocked. She didn't know anyone in Greece. "Who's hosting it?" She thought of the only faint possibility. "Not your sister?"

"No." He chewed and swallowed a bite of bacon, washing it down with more hot black coffee. "I might have another chance at Paris. I'm hoping to discuss it tonight."

At first Emmie thought he hadn't answered her question. Then she realized he had.

"*The* Paris project?" she said. "The one we've chased for years? The property owned by Pierre Harcourt?"

Theo nodded. "There are rumors that he's not happy with the new development team."

"Harcourt is hosting a reception for us?"

Theo pushed his food around his plate with his fork, then said reluctantly, "His daughter."

Emmie blinked, suddenly feeling a slight chill across the yacht's deck, even beneath the warm Greek sun. "Your old girlfriend?"

He shrugged. "Ancient history. Long before your time."

"Celine Harcourt? The one who smashed a plate on your head at Per Se?"

"She smashed it against the wall, at Le Bernardin. Though she was aiming at my head." His lips twisted humorously. "Celine didn't take rejection well."

She hid the tremble of her hands as she set her linen napkin on the table. "No one does."

Theo's handsome face lifted in a sudden grin. "Jealous?"

She muttered under her breath. He leaned forward, taking both her hands in his own.

"You have nothing to worry about," he said. "You're the only woman I want. Forever and ever."

She searched his gaze, her heart pounding. "Am I?"

His head tilted, his expression turning wicked. "Well. Let me think." He kissed the back of her hand, then the other. "Perhaps…" turning the hands over, he kissed her palm "…I should…" he kissed the other palm "…be certain…"

Taking her finger in his mouth, he suckled it, swirling her fingertip with his tongue, as he'd done so expertly to other parts of her that were even more sensitive.

She shivered at the wet heat of his mouth. Her nipples were hard as desire coiled inside her. Pulling her finger from his mouth with one last kiss, he rose unsteadily to his feet.

"Now I know you'll join me…" He lifted dark eyebrows with a crooked grin. "I'm going for a swim." His powerful legs shifted as he turned on the yacht's deck. "Catch me if you can."

Without warning, he ran straight off the edge of the deck, falling the long distance. She heard a splash far below, against the hard sapphire surface of the water.

Emmie caught her breath. Standing up so fast she felt dizzy, she rushed to the edge to look down.

He was swimming in the water, totally unconcerned about any danger, his slick, wet dark hair shining in the sun. He laughed when he saw her face. "There's nothing for you to be scared of. Come in. The water's fine."

Later that night, Theo sat beside Emmie on the speedboat en route to Santorini, his arm around her. He could not remember the last time he'd felt so relaxed, so sated, so... He didn't know how to describe it.

The summer sun was lowering fast over the Aegean, turning it the color of Homer's wine-colored water. Ahead, he could see the lights of Oia shining in the twilight.

But it was nothing compared to the way his wife glowed.

Theo looked down at her. The red sequins of her short dress shimmered as the boat swayed and leaped over the waves of Amoudi Bay. Her long hair, streaked with honey highlights from their time in the sun, flew behind her, and she'd added a hint of makeup to her flushed, pretty face. His gaze fell to her bare legs beneath the short hemline, her pedicured feet in strappy high heels, her toenails glistening baby pink.

As the vintage wood speedboat flew across the water, her full breasts, pressed into deep cleavage by lingerie, bounced with every hard wave. He tried not to look. Tried and failed and wanted her even now, even though they'd made love three times today, just since they'd gone swimming in the sea.

Would he ever get enough of her?

Emmie's rosy lips suddenly curved, and he knew he'd been caught. He looked up guiltily, but she smiled, her eyes bright.

Something twisted in his heart.

She was just so beautiful, whether in a designer gown, a cheap sundress, or nothing. Naked was his preference.

Two hours earlier, when they were still lazing in bed, Emmie had rolled her eyes when he suggested that for the reception tonight, she wear one of the designer dresses the New York stylist had packed into her trousseau. Reaching for a silk robe to cover her luscious body, Emmie had ducked her head. "Couldn't we just skip the whole thing?"

"I'm afraid we must go," he said, a little remorsefully. Rising from the bed, Theo had stretched his limbs with pleasure after hours of lovemaking. "When Celine heard we were in Greece on our honeymoon, she was nice enough to throw us a party. Plus, I want to find out about Paris."

Emmie's violet-blue eyes were luminous as she pleaded, "You could go without me."

Theo frowned, bemused. "Why wouldn't you want to come? Her father's house is beautiful, the most glamorous on Thira."

Instead of looking pleased, her lips sagged at the edges. She whispered, "I won't fit in."

"That's true." Pulling her close, he'd nestled her body against his own, with only the thin silk of her robe between them. Kissing her neck, he'd gently tugged open the neckline as he whispered, "You're more beautiful than any of them."

Her silk brushed against his skin as he'd pulled her back into bed.

Later, as he followed her out of the shower, he found Emmie wet and naked, digging frantically through her heretofore untouched designer wardrobe now hanging in the yacht bedroom's closet. Surrounded by piles of lovely dresses on the floor, she'd begged him for help.

And he'd given it to her. Oh, how he'd given it to her.

He'd helped her pick out a dress, too.

Now, as their speedboat grew closer to the island, he could make out the magnificent mansion owned by Celine's father. Built a hundred years before, the classical architecture looked slightly out of place, a miniature Versailles dropped willy-nilly onto a Greek island. Other boats already filled the marina. He saw shadows of people arriving, heard the low hum of music and conversation across the water.

Glancing at his wife, he saw she too was staring at the mansion. Her expression was scared. He squeezed her hand.

"The most beautiful one there," he repeated.

She flashed him a grateful look, then looked him over in his tuxedo. "You're not so bad yourself."

It was full twilight, and the moon had just started to rise, as Theo helped her out of the boat onto the enormous dock, lit up by fairy lights. His gaze raked over Emmie in the sparkling red dress, showing off her sensual shape. So pregnant, so sexy, all woman—

A curse went through his brain. How could he want her again already? he thought with wonder.

The three times he'd made love to her today had been explosive, as always, and yet something had been different. Had it been the sunlight? The sea?

Or was it because, three days ago, for the first time in

his life, he'd opened up to a woman and revealed something no one else knew?

His body, which had been so relaxed, suddenly tensed.

Had he made a mistake? Had he told her too much about his past? Had he sounded like he was complaining? Like he was weak? Had he said anything that she could somehow use against him?

And he hadn't even shared the worst of his past. He couldn't. Not even with her.

Especially not with her.

If Emmie ever knew the truth—

His heart suddenly felt like it was going to explode out of his chest.

She won't, he told himself. Let the past stay buried. Like their mother's old locket, now smothered beneath the earth on Lyra.

Theo Papadopolous was gone. He'd been born Theo Katrakis at sixteen, when he came to America and became his uncle's heir. He was rich and powerful now. No one could ever hurt him. Cold. He was cold. He had no feelings.

But as his wife clutched his arm, smiling up at him, her eyes shining in the fiery torches lighting up the Santorini hillside, his heart loped in his chest. And he felt the first stirrings of fear. What would happen if Emmie ever really knew?

CHAPTER NINE

EMMIE CLUNG TO her husband's arm as they walked past the torches that led along the path from the dock to the sprawling Baroque mansion, a wedding-cake confection of pink and white, clinging to the hillside above the shore. She felt cold in the warm summer night.

A soft sea breeze blew against her overheated skin, brushing over the red sequins of her sleeveless cocktail dress. The rectangular paillettes shimmered beneath the mansion's lights flooding from the windows, the sequins similar in size and sparkle to the ten-karat emerald-cut diamond on her left hand.

She glanced nervously to the right and left. She saw others arriving who looked elegant and yet casual, in body-conscious beige or black, as if a soiree in a twenty-million-euro mansion in Santorini was just another Thursday night. All Emmie wanted was to fit in. To not embarrass her husband.

To not make him wonder why he'd married her and wish he hadn't.

But it was hard for Emmie, as they walked through grand double doors, and uniformed servers offered champagne from silver trays, not to feel like she was out of step and out of her league.

The other guests had been born into fortune or earned it

themselves. Some were special for their athletic prowess, others for their cleverness, others for their beauty.

But Emmie? All she'd done was get herself knocked up.

As they entered the ballroom—a *ballroom*, in someone's private house!—she glanced nervously at Theo. Now *he* fit in all right. He looked gorgeous, his powerfully muscled body civilized by his well-tailored tuxedo. He looked handsome and cold.

Only she knew the depths of emotion and darkness in his soul.

But you don't know, a voice whispered inside her. *You're afraid to know.*

"It's something, isn't it?" Theo flashed her a crooked smile as he looked up at the frescoes on the ceilings above.

"Something," she echoed. Sipping a glass of juice, she glanced around uncertainly. She felt people looking at them, whispering.

"Celine's great-grandfather built this place before the First World War." He added wryly, "Sometimes I feel like that's how long I've been pitching her father about his Paris property."

"How many times have you tried?"

"At least five times. The first was years ago, before I met you. Before I knew Nico, even." His eyes sharpened. "Ah. There she is."

He pulled her forward to a petite, very slender blonde, wearing a simple beige dress with straps and no embellishment.

"Theo." Coming forward, the Frenchwoman lifted on the toes of her stilettos to kiss one of his cheeks, then the other.

"Thank you for throwing us a party," he said, smiling as he looked around the crowded ballroom.

Celine dropped back with a pout, teasingly hitting the

lapel of his tuxedo jacket with her hand. "Though, why I should be so good to you, when you never even bothered to invite me to your wedding, I cannot imagine. Hello." She turned the force of her attention to Emmie. "So you are the lucky Mrs. Katrakis."

A moment before, thanks to Theo's compliments, Emmie had been feeling almost pretty. But now, compared to the small, slender French heiress, Emmie suddenly felt as grotesque as a red disco ball—shiny, round and vulgar.

"I am happy to make your acquaintance," she stammered in schoolgirl French. Sadly, it sounded nothing like when she'd practiced in the yacht earlier that afternoon. Her words sounded garbled, like she had marbles in her mouth.

Celine looked startled, then her smile sharpened. She gave Emmie two cheek kisses in response, then said airily, "Enjoy your party."

Cheeks hot, Emmie glanced quickly at Theo, feeling like she'd made a fool of herself. He was watching Celine go.

"Theo."

He turned to her. "Shall I introduce you to everyone?"

But she'd seen the way his eyes had lingered on his ex-girlfriend. She wondered what he was thinking, but then thought that maybe this, too, was something she was afraid to know.

For the next hour Theo introduced her to the wealthy, famous, fabulous people who were his peers and Celine's. Emmie duly shook hands with or was air-kissed by tycoons, government leaders, movie stars and nepo babies.

"Congratulations," they all said to her, as they looked from gorgeous Theo in his well-cut tuxedo to Emmie's flushed face and pregnant belly. And as their lips curved, she knew what they were thinking because she was thinking the same: she didn't deserve to be here.

She met a few more celebrities, followed by harried assistants. Looking at the assistants, Emmie felt sympathy. She almost wished she could be here as Theo's secretary instead of his wife. At least then she'd know how to behave and could go unnoticed. How she missed it now, the simple sweetness of being invisible!

After a few minutes of standing idly by, as Theo spoke to two other men, their conversation switching rapidly between English, Italian and Spanish, Emmie finally murmured "Excuse me" and wandered to the buffet table.

Quietly, she made herself a plate of hors d'oeuvres and drank sparkling water. Going to stand in a corner, she munched her food and watched as the behavior of the guests steadily deteriorated across the ballroom. As the evening grew late, they drank to excess and screamed laughter and kissed one person then another, making Emmie wonder if they'd taken drugs in the palatial bathrooms or if she'd fallen headlong into a Roman orgy.

She suddenly wished she was back home, in Queens, attending a potluck with her neighbors and friends who actually cared about each other, more than shocking or impressing or competing with rivals and frenemies.

"Madame Katrakis."

Turning, she saw Celine Harcourt. Her throat went tight, but she gave her best attempt at a smile. "Call me Emmie. Please."

The slim blonde gave a cool smile. "Thank you." She made no suggestion that Emmie should similarly call her Celine. "My dear, you look terribly bored. You must let me entertain you."

"No, I—"

"This way," the Frenchwoman said, and with no good excuse to slight the hostess Emmie set down her plate and followed her, through a secret door that required a code, and up a slender flight of stairs to a quiet alcove above the ballroom.

Emmie looked down and saw the entire party below: the band, people dancing, gossiping, couples making out in corners, all the whirl of beautiful people and beautiful clothes.

"Disgusting, isn't it?" Celine sighed, standing beside her. "My father built this balcony so if he fancied some girl, he could bring her up here and make love to her, without having to miss his party. And, of course, so that he could immediately kick her out afterward, with none the wiser."

As Emmie turned to her with shocked eyes, the Frenchwoman lit a cigarette from a pack resting on the small sofa nearby.

"You are far from home, are you not, little secretary?" As she shook out the match, her gaze fell on Emmie's belly beneath the red sequin dress. "You got the golden ticket, and now you are his wife. How did you do it? A hole in the condom? Pretending to be on the pill?"

"Uh…"

"He should have been mine." Celine's eyes looked out toward the spot in the ballroom where Theo was still talking intensely to the two other tycoons. "But I thought it the decent thing to wait six months, at least, before I forced his hand." Her gaze fell back to Emmie's belly. "More fool me."

"It wasn't like that," Emmie protested. "I never tricked him."

She inhaled her cigarette, holding it elegantly, exhaling smoke before she gave a cold smile. "Didn't you?"

The horrible woman tried to make it sound as if Emmie had gotten pregnant on purpose—which she hadn't!

Had she?

After Theo had kissed her on Mount Corcovado at the

base of the lit-up statue, she had little memory of the passionate, steamy ride back to Ipanema Beach. She just remembered how she'd trembled as he led her back to his hotel suite.

She'd returned his kiss desperately, with clumsy inexperience, as he'd lowered her to the enormous bed. They ripped off each other's clothes, kissing and tasting and teasing each other until she was gasping with need, until he finally, with agonizing slowness, pushed himself inside her.

She'd felt a sharp pain then, but he'd kissed her, slowly wooing and luring her, until she again felt only pleasure. It was only when she'd finally cried out her fulfillment that he'd finally let himself go.

"There was never any question of…of…" Her cheeks were burning. "We—neither of us—um, we just didn't think about it."

Celine blinked, staring at her blankly, letting her cigarette burn to ash. Then her thin eyebrows lowered. "Do you mean to tell me that Theo just…forgot about birth control? *Theo?*"

This was getting weird. "It's really none of your business," Emmie said, backing away. "Thank you for hosting this party for us, it's so very kind, but I should really get back to my husband now."

Drawing herself up with as much dignity as she could muster, Emmie turned to go.

"You're not good enough for him. Nowhere near good enough." Celine's lovely face was contorted with bewildered rage. She took a puff of her cigarette with a shaking hand. "You? The fat little secretary? You should never be anything but a servant, raising his child, serving his needs, counting out the days till you're paid-off."

Emmie gasped at her rudeness. "That is—"

"You might have convinced him to marry you," Celine interrupted. "But he'll never love you. You know that, don't you?" When she saw Emmie's agonized face, she relaxed and smiled. She took another long drag on her cigarette, then exhaled. "Enjoy the party while it lasts, little secretary."

"So it's true," the Italian said.

"What?" Theo said.

The Spaniard lifted an amused eyebrow, his gaze focused just past Theo's ear. "You have a wife."

"So?" Turning, Theo saw Emmie, following their hostess through the crowded ballroom uncertainly.

Hmm, he thought. Never a good thing to have one's wife comparing notes with one's ex-mistress, even though his relationship with Celine had ended years before. He consoled himself with the thought that there wasn't anything the Frenchwoman could say—that Theo was arrogant, that he was selfish—that Emmie didn't already know. In spades.

His gaze lingered on his wife's sexy shape in the red sparkling dress, at her lovely face as she bit her lower lip in consternation, wobbling a bit in her high heels. A smile traced his lips. Adorable.

"I could hardly believe it," the Italian, Giovanni Orsini, drawled. He took a sip of scotch. "Such a choice."

"I mean, honor is all very *well*, in theory," Carlos Mondragón agreed, "but a little goes a long way."

The three tycoons, acquaintances who saw each other a few times a year, had been discussing sports, mostly cricket and tennis, in spite of Theo's best efforts to work the conversation around to real-estate development in general and

Harcourt's property in particular. Now, he blinked at them in bewilderment. "What are you talking about?"

The other men glanced at each other.

"Your marriage," said Giovanni.

"To your secretary," said Carlos.

Theo stiffened. "What about it?"

"You were correct to support the child, and the mother, of course," the Italian said. "But *marriage*? To a secretary?"

"I didn't take you for a snob, Orsini."

He shrugged with an easy smile. "Love affairs are all very well, and accidents *will* happen, if one isn't careful. But marriage is a serious business for men of our station. And taking a mere secretary as your wife... It's hardly the way to start a dynasty, is it?"

Theo was still stinging from Orsini's casual criticism of *if one isn't careful* when he was distracted by that insulting dismissal of Emmie. Hearing his wife, with all her beauty and gorgeously kind heart, described as a *mere secretary* filled Theo with sudden, breathless rage. His hands clenched, and he nearly punched his friend.

But why? Why would Orsini's words make him so angry, when they were obviously true?

What the hell was wrong with him?

Cold, Theo ordered himself. Ice-cold.

He forced himself to turn to the Spaniard, who'd gone quiet. "And you, Mondragón? You agree with this?"

The man shrugged. "As someone who nearly was caught myself recently, all I can say is I was lucky to escape." Gulping down the rest of his scotch, he gave a smile that didn't meet his eyes. "Only a fool marries for love."

Love? Even the word seemed like a judgment to Theo. Love was the worst kind of weakness. "It's not a question of *love*," he defended. "Emmie's pregnant with my son. He must have the protection of my name, and so will she."

"Very noble."

"Very," said Carlos Mondragón, signaling for another drink.

Theo set his jaw, growing more annoyed by the moment. "If it ever happens to you, you'll understand."

"No accidental children for me. I make sure."

"I make *very* sure," Giovanni Orsini added smugly.

"Talk to me if you become a father. Until then, remain silent about what you don't understand," Theo bit out. "If a man does not take care of his own child, he is not a man."

The other two looked at each other.

"True enough," the Italian was forced to concede.

Carlos Mondragón shook his head impatiently. "The subject grows tedious. Let's talk business." Looking both ways in the crowded ballroom, he leaned forward and whispered, "It's true. Pierre Harcourt's looking for a new developer."

Theo sucked in his breath. "For Paris?"

Taking a new scotch off a waiter's tray, Carlos nodded.

He tried to hide the sudden pounding of his heart. The famous Harcourt property in Paris, one of the last undeveloped big parcels in the heart of the city, had been his dream for years. It was how he'd first met Celine Harcourt, years ago, while pitching development plans to her father. Even tonight, he'd stared at her, wondering how to ask if the rumor he'd heard could be true.

Pierre Harcourt was a difficult man to please. For years, the man had dragged his feet on pulling the trigger and developing a property that had belonged to his aristocratic ancestors before they were hauled off on tumbrels.

But Theo had never given up. He'd been dazzled by the potential, from the moment he'd seen the vast car park on the edge of the Seine. Emmie had helped him with that last proposal, when he'd spent millions of euros on architectural and landscape design, investigating government regulations and wooing potential investors. It had all seemed wasted when Harcourt chose a different firm last year.

Until now.

"What about Allmond?"

"Financing fell through. I heard from my mistress whose cousin works there. Harcourt is now looking for stability and deep pockets." Snorting, the Italian saluted him with his lowball glass. "Clearly describes you now, old man."

Theo ignored the teasing. "Is it public knowledge?"

"It will be, tomorrow."

"Is Harcourt here?" Theo demanded, looking sharply around the ballroom.

"You think he'd attend one of his daughter's bacchanals? He's past that these days. He's in Paris—hey, where are you going?"

Theo had departed without farewell, looking for his wife.

Pushing through the drunken crowds in the ballroom, he finally saw Emmie, bountiful and sexy, a gorgeous red flame amid tiny wispy women in beige slip dresses. Even without red sequins, Emmie would have shone for him like a star.

But her shoulders seemed slumped, and she seemed to stumble in her strappy stilettos. Should he have tried harder to include her in his discussion with the two men? But Theo knew she wasn't a fan of sports, and he'd thought her unlikely to be mesmerized by discussion of the summer cricket season, conducted half in Spanish and Italian. So he hadn't been surprised when she'd wandered away to the buffet table.

But now, he set his jaw grimly. Had Celine said something rude?

There was a loud cheer around them, as the clock struck midnight, and as always at Celine's summer parties, the music changed from classical quintet to pulsing, soaring club music arranged by a famous DJ who charged hundreds of thousands a night. All around them, wealthy, beautiful people poured onto the ballroom floor, as multicolor lights flashed around them.

Their eyes locked across the crowded ballroom. His wife shimmered like a dream, as the beat and haunting melody lifted him to a strange euphoria.

Emmie.

His mouth went dry as something tightened in his chest.

Shaking himself out of his trance, he set his jaw and went grimly through the crowd. When he reached her, he thought she looked pale. He wanted to ask what Celine had said to her, but instead he said merely, "We should go."

"Okay," she said quietly. Maybe she was just tired? He wanted to believe that. He took her arm, in case she needed support, with those damned high heels causing her such trouble. With his other hand, he reached into his tuxedo jacket pocket for his phone.

They left the hillside mansion, overlooking the moonswept sea. He helped her walk down the path, beneath flickering red lights. The vintage 1950s speedboat pulled up before the two of them even reached the end of the dock. His drivers prided themselves on being quick.

As the boat hurried back toward his anchored yacht, Theo sat in the long back seat beside Emmie, his arm stretched behind her.

"I have some bad news," he told her in a low voice, over the roar of the engine and splash of the wake.

Her big eyes shimmered at him in the moonlight. "What?"

He took her smaller hand in his own. "I'm afraid we'll have to miss Mykonos and cut our honeymoon short."

"Why?" She swallowed, then whispered, "What changed your mind?"

Lifting her hand to his mouth, he kissed it gently. He felt her shiver, just from that, and it made him want... But there was no time for that, he thought with real regret. "I need to go to Paris. Pierre Harcourt's deal with Allmond fell through."

"Paris!" She sucked in her breath, her lovely face filled with shock, then delight. He smiled, touched that she knew what it meant to him. He did not have to explain. She wanted him to have it.

"The yacht will go full speed to Paros, where my jet will be gassed up and waiting to take me to Paris."

"Paros to Paris," she laughed. Then the light in her eyes faded. "Taking you? Just you?"

Still holding her hand, Theo looked up at his approaching yacht, its lit-up windows illuminating Santorini's dark sea. He looked down at their entwined hands barely visible in the moonlight.

"It's going to take all my energy to work up a new pitch," he said in a low voice. "I'll be working sixteen-hour days for the next month."

"*Eighteen*-hour days," she corrected.

She knew him too well. He gave her a crooked smile. "Eighteen."

"Why not bring me with you?" she said slowly. "You know I could help."

He knew. He'd never had a better secretary—ever. She'd been his protector, his partner, his friend. "I can't."

"Why?" she demanded.

Swallowing the temptation, he shook his head. "As you said. You're not my secretary. I promised you'd live in New York, close to family and friends. Plus, you're pregnant."

"So?"

"So?" He stared at her incredulously. "You can't work eighteen-hour days."

"Don't tell me what I can do." Emmie stroked her cheek thoughtfully. "You think developing the pitch will take a month?"

"Or longer," he was forced to admit. "And you'll want to be home, comfortable and safe, with people you love, not bored and alone at the George V, or working at the office till you drop. No." He gave a regretful smile. "I'll leave tonight while you're sleeping on the yacht. As soon as I reach Paris, I'll send the jet back to Paros. When you wake tomorrow, it will take you home."

She stubbornly focused on the point. "Maybe it will be easier than you think. We still have the pitch from last year."

"Harcourt already heard that and rejected it. We have to rethink the pitch entirely. It needs to be visionary. I'll send for additional staff from London and New York." He thought of sending for Edna and shuddered. "I'll get a secretary from the agency. But just being first to pitch isn't enough. This time we'll focus on dazzling not just Old Man Harcourt but also his daughter."

"Daughter." Her gaze darkened. "Celine will be there?"

He shrugged. "She's his only child. He values her opinion." In fact, he valued it too much, in Theo's opinion. Celine didn't give a damn about the property, just the money it would provide her.

Emmie looked out at the moonlit sea and seemed to shiver. No wonder she was cold, with her arms, legs and neckline so bare. He wrapped his arm around her shoulders, forcing his gaze not to linger on the swell of her breasts. No. He wouldn't even look.

"I'll miss your expertise." He quirked a wicked smile. "And a few other things." She wouldn't even meet his glance. He sighed. "Once you're in New York, maybe you could look over the list of secretaries we get from the agency. At least if you approve—"

Emmie turned her head sharply. "I'm coming with you to Paris."

Theo blinked. "What?"

"I'll be your secretary. Just like before."

But you're not my secretary anymore, Theo knew he should say. *You're my wife.*

Something held him back. Having Emmie as his secretary would make it more likely he'd achieve his objective.

Having her as his wife would burn his nights like fire.

"Are you…sure?" he said slowly. "It's really what you want?"

Emmie tilted her head, looking at him beneath the sweep of her dark eyelashes as a little smile played over her red lips. "You're too much to handle for any secretary but me."

"True," he said, amused. He felt a rush of gratitude. "Thank you, Emmie," he said quietly. "You don't know what this means to me."

"I know." Their eyes locked, and his heart skipped a beat.

He pulled her close, wrapping her in both arms, against his chest. Pressed against his white tuxedo shirt, her full breasts seemed barely contained by the sequined neckline, the spaghetti straps about to snap. It was all he could do not to snap them off himself.

All he wanted to do was kiss her, but Yiannis was just now pulling the speedboat close to the yacht. There was no time—

With an intake of breath, he looked at her. "We have two hours before we'll reach my plane in Paros."

"Right." She started to pull away, suddenly all business. "I'll start pulling up research, then call the Paris office—"

"Later," Theo whispered and lowered his head to kiss her.

CHAPTER TEN

"YOU'RE DONE," Theo said suddenly one evening in their Paris office. "I'm taking you out."

"Done?" Emmie looked up blearily from three separate computer screens spread over her desk, showing all the final details of the Harcourt proposal. "What do you mean? We still have—"

Theo gently pulled a stylus from one of her hands and an electronic tablet from the other. "We've done everything we can. We can leave the cleanup and polishing to the team." He looked around the office. "Right, team?"

"We got it, boss," came the cheerful replies in French and English.

Emmie blinked owlishly, disoriented after twelve straight hours of focus. She looked around her. With its cream-colored walls, gilt-framed paintings and old-wood parquet floors, the Katrakis Paris office was very different from the New York office's glass and steel. The nineteenth-century building was in the Étoile district with a view of the Arc de Triomphe. The floor could hold twenty employees comfortably, but was currently bursting at the seams with thirty-two, including the extra staff flown in from London and New York.

For the last month, they'd been working all-out on this

proposal—crunching numbers, collating technical and legal data, and creating a beautiful, eye-popping presentation, which they'd show Pierre Harcourt and his daughter tomorrow morning.

Now heavily pregnant, Emmie was finding it a little harder to make it through the sixteen-hour workdays, especially since every night, during time she should have spent sleeping, she made love to her husband once or twice. She didn't regret it. How could she resist Theo's touch, which was like an intoxicating fire?

But still. She'd be glad when the Katrakis team formally presented their proposal tomorrow at Harcourt's office in La Défense. Theo was certain it would immediately succeed. Emmie was less certain. She suspected the Harcourts would request modifications, playing their offer against sales pitches of rivals, in give-and-take of negotiations that could take weeks, if not longer.

She hoped she was wrong and Theo was right. She loved the thought of returning to New York tomorrow night. She yearned for a good night's sleep, for the baby's sake if not for hers, and the chance to nap a little and put up her swollen feet. And to see her family again.

The Swensons were all doing well. Her brothers had all moved out of the family apartment, but Karl was hardly lonely as he and her two older brothers spent their days expanding Swenson and Sons Plumbing. Her second youngest brother, Sam, at twenty-one, had registered for nursing school and was living with his girlfriend in Jersey City. Daniel, the youngest at nineteen, had just departed for Oklahoma to study cybersecurity at the University of Tulsa. Emmie smiled. Call it the Theo Katrakis Scholarship Fund.

Her friends were doing well, too. Honora was pregnant again, and she'd promised to throw Emmie and Theo a baby shower when they were back in New York. Emmie could hardly wait.

But she'd given her word to Theo to help him achieve his dream. She intended to see it through. All she wanted was for him to be happy, because she—

Because she—

"I'm fine," she told Theo briskly, even as her stomach growled and her knees shook with exhaustion. "I don't need special treatment. I can finish."

"There's no question of special treatment, Emmie. You've fought harder than anyone." Theo's warm black eyes smiled down at her, his gaze like a caress.

This was why she'd worked so hard, she thought. A lump rose in her throat. For *him*. For the last month, she'd thrown herself into being the perfect wife and perfect secretary because she'd yearned to see Theo look at her like this for just one precious moment. With approval. With admiration. With...

Love?

Catching her breath, she shook her head. "I'll stay."

Theo's eyes flickered with respect, then he came closer, drawing her away to a quiet corner, away from the efficient, chattering employees crowding around the screens.

"Remember Rio?" he said softly.

Her lips lifted on the edges. Putting her hands over the full swell of her belly, she said, "Um, yes?"

He snorted, then his eyes grew serious. "You accused me of being a brute of a boss, never allowing you to leave the office even when we traveled around the world. And you were right. So tonight, before we leave France," he took her hand, "I want you to see the City of Lights. To celebrate our coming triumph."

Her eyebrows lifted at the word *triumph*. "Aren't you the one who always says never to count on success?"

"This time is different."

"How do you know?"

He shrugged. "I feel it."

"There are other developers offering proposals, good ones—"

"They'll lose. We'll win." He lowered his head. She felt his lips brush against her ear as he said, huskily, "Let's celebrate."

When he pulled back, his dark eyes caught hers, and she shivered.

"All right," she whispered.

Looking around the office, Theo called, "See you tomorrow at Harcourt's office."

His employees' answering cheer swelled around them, and he responded with a salute. Handing Emmie her sleek new Hermès Birkin bag, he led her to the building's antique birdcage elevator. As they descended, he gave her a sideways glance.

"What is it?" she said, gripping the handle of her bag, beige like her Prada shoes.

"I was just thinking how amazing the last month has been."

"It has."

"And I was thinking, maybe—" He gave a rueful chuckle as they reached the ground floor. "We can talk about it later."

But as they walked through the lobby, Emmie had a feeling he was glad to put off whatever he'd been about to say. Strange. It wasn't like Theo to procrastinate over anything. He was usually like a bull in a china shop, plowing forward with whatever he wanted.

"*Bonsoir, Madame* Katrakis…*monsieur*," the doorman said.

"*Bonsoir*, Jérémie," Emmie replied, holding Theo's arm in his tailored jacket.

She dimly heard the click-click-click of her heels beside his heavier footstep on the marble floor. As he led her out the door to the tree-lined Paris avenue, she looked up at him dreamily. He was darkly handsome, powerful and ruthless in his tailored Italian suit. And she was dressed to match.

Madame Katrakis.

In her cream silk shirt and camel cashmere skirt over her baby bump, wedding pearls in her ears and huge emerald-cut diamond on her left hand, Emmie now looked the part of a billionaire's wife.

When they'd arrived in Paris, Theo had insisted she must have a new, chic wardrobe. "You need the proper armor, Emmie," he'd told her, "to fight at my side in the most glamorous city in the world."

Thinking of Celine Harcourt, Emmie had reluctantly agreed, and a stylist had arrived at their four-story town house that very hour. Her closet was now filled with clothes of quiet, understated luxury: fine fabrics, perfect fit, a total lack of designer logos, and colors that varied between black, white and beige. Every morning at six for the last month, a hairstylist had duly arrived, to blow out Emmie's honey-blond hair and make it sleek and glossy, as makeup was discreetly applied.

Et voilà. Armor.

Theo hadn't been wrong. Emmie saw the respect her costume created in other people. So it was almost worth it, feeling trapped in tight, unforgiving seams, washed out in bland and boring colors, and so hot in the blast of July in Paris.

Once she was back in New York, Emmie promised herself, it would all go straight into the penthouse closet. After this, she intended to finish her pregnancy in loose sundresses, stretchy T-shirts and maternity shorts. She would sleep twelve hours a night or maybe more.

"I'm thinking about tomorrow," Theo said abruptly as they walked a short distance along the avenue.

"About the presentation?" Emmie stopped on the sidewalk. "Should we go back?"

"No. Not that." He licked his lips. "It's about our return to New York."

"What about it?" They'd arranged for a concierge doctor to chaperone their flight, with Emmie so close to her due date. She gave him a reassuring smile. "It'll be all right if the negotiations delay us a few days. One of the good things about owning a private jet. No extra fees for changing one's schedule."

Theo stared at her for a moment, then looked past her. "Ah. There he is."

Their gleaming Bentley was waiting for them at the curb a little way down, a chauffeur standing beside the open back door. As they walked, Emmie took a deep breath of fresh air. How lovely to be out of the office.

And in Paris. Just past the leafy green trees and stately cream-colored buildings with pale blue shutters, she could see the grandeur of the Arc de Triomphe at the end of the avenue turning pink as the sun was starting to set to the west. As they climbed into the back of the waiting Bentley, the chauffeur closing the door behind them, the leather felt smooth and sensual beneath the bare hollows of her knees.

"Where are we going?" she asked her husband.

"Dinner first." Theo kissed the back of her hand, his lips like fire. His dark eyes burned through her. "I hope you're hungry."

"Starving," she whispered.

"Good." His expression as he looked down at her made her throat tight.

Did she see more than desire in his dark eyes? More than approval for her secretarial skills?

Was it possible that Theo actually—

"He'll never love you. You know that, don't you?"

Celine's spiteful words echoed in her mind, and her brief hope faded.

Emmie had never had reason to be jealous of the French-woman. She knew that now. Theo's interest in Celine was the same that he had in Pierre Harcourt. To him, they were nothing but indecisive property owners who needed to be convinced to choose Katrakis Enterprises as their real-estate developer.

But that wasn't enough. Celine wasn't the problem.

It was those words. Because Emmie feared—no, she knew—that they were true.

For the last month, Emmie had tried to distract herself from that fact. She'd worked past the point of exhaustion until the pregnancy hormones that amplified her emotions became flattened out and sleepy. She'd allowed herself no time to think, no time to feel.

But now, as their driver took them through Paris, she had no numbers to crunch or images to collate. As her husband held her hand, pointing out the sparkle of the Eiffel Tower at sunset and the silhouette of Notre Dame's famous gargoyles, black against the red twilight, Emmie suddenly felt everything. Including the reason she'd worked so long and hard the last month in Paris to be the perfect wife and secretary. Why she was so desperately trying to win his approval and esteem.

She was in love with him.

In spite of all her efforts, in spite of knowing Theo for the selfish, arrogant cad he could be, Emmie had foolishly given her heart to the complicated man who was her husband.

A man who desired her, and who appreciated her secretarial skills, but had no capacity for love. As he'd told her from the start. She suddenly blinked back tears. Was there any hope?

Following their chauffeured visits to the most unabashedly touristy attractions of the city, Theo surprised her with dinner for two on a private cruise down the Seine.

"I set this up myself." Theo gave a proud smile. He never arranged logistical details himself. When she didn't respond, his smile faded. "But if you don't like it, I could get us a late-night reservation at le Café de la Paix—"

"A dinner cruise, I love it," she forced herself to say.

And she did try to enjoy it. But as they sat on the deck and enjoyed a private dinner for two by candlelight, floating down the Seine as they watched the dreamy lights of Paris go by in the darkness, for some reason she felt like crying.

Theo's handsome face was bewildered as he looked down at her barely touched plate. "Is something wrong with the food?"

"No, it's delicious," she said and choked down several bites of rich chateaubriand in truffle sauce, the buttery cheeses, the flaky orange blossom tart, washing it down with sparkling, rose-infused water.

At midnight, their chauffeur drove them back to the eighteenth-century *hôtel particulier* on the Île Saint-Louis overlooking the Seine, which Theo had rented from a penurious aristocrat at exorbitant cost. He punched in the ten-digit security code at the tall iron gate, drawing her into the small dark garden as the gate closed behind them with a clang.

"My God, you're beautiful," Theo said huskily. His dark eyes moved over her in the white silk blouse and camel skirt. "I've wanted to do this all night—"

He lowered his mouth to hers beneath the streetlights dappled through the trees. Pressing her against the wrought iron fence, he kissed her hungrily. As his tongue swept hers, electrifying her senses, she clung to him with equal need.

Drawing her to the imposing front door, he punched in another security code, then led her inside the grand home.

Yanking off his suit jacket, he dropped it to the checkered marble floor and led her up the wide, sweeping staircase with its decorative iron curlicues, in a palace built for noblemen long ago for a life long since vanished.

Leading her to the master bedroom, Theo looked at her in the semidarkness, illuminated only by faint moonlight and the passing river traffic below. He pulled off her silk blouse, revealing full breasts overflowing the white lacy bra. Falling to his knees with an intake of breath, he slowly unzipped the back of her cashmere skirt, and that, too, dropped to the priceless Turkish rug. He looked up, past her white lace panties and the swell of her pregnant belly, past her full breasts. His dark eyes locked with hers.

She shivered, looking down at him. Shadows played against his high cheekbones, crooked aquiline nose and dark scruff of his jawline. His ruthlessly handsome face was stark with need.

Rising to his feet, he gently lowered her back against the large four-poster bed. He pulled off her high heels, one by one, kissing the insole of each foot before he tossed the designer shoe to the floor. Moving over her, he slowly stroked her, pulling off first her bra, then her panties.

Backing up, he removed his platinum cuff links, placing them carefully on the nightstand with a clink. His dark eyes never left hers as he kicked off his gleaming leather shoes, unbuttoned his tailored shirt, removed his trousers and silk boxers, dropping it all to the floor.

Her husband stood in front of her, naked and unashamed. Emmie's mouth went dry as her eyes roamed down his powerful chest and arms, to his muscled thighs, laced with dark hair, all the way to his scarred ankle. Then the sacred place in the middle, hard and ready for her. Aching with need, she wordlessly held out her arms.

He made love to her passionately in the mansion overlooking the Seine, carefully pulling her up to ride him. He overwhelmed her with pleasure as he'd done every night from the moment they'd wed.

But this time was different.

Afterward, Theo held her in the moonlight, their bodies sweaty in the warm breeze off the river from the open balcony. Her head rested against his bare chest as he caressed her hair.

And she quietly wept.

Now she knew she loved him. And worse.

Emmie wanted him to love her back, for their marriage to be based on more than just parenthood, more than partnership, more than even sex. She wanted love that lasted forever.

Theo's hand froze as he stroked her wet cheek. "What's this?" He frowned down at her in the dim light. "Tears?"

"No," she lied. Turning, she pressed her face to his skin.

"Emmie?" Sitting up, he sounded worried. "What's wrong?"

"Nothing."

"You're overtired. I've been working you too hard." She

didn't answer. He took a deep breath. "You're missing your family," he said quietly. "You're homesick."

Their bodies were still entwined on the shadowy bed, but she'd never felt so far apart.

Emmie lifted her head from his chest. His black eyes pierced her soul, whispering of the pain waiting for her, loving someone for the rest of her life who'd never love her back. She looked toward the open balcony, toward the lowering dark clouds shrouding the Parisian night sky.

"Yes," she whispered. She looked at him. "Don't you want to go home?"

Home.

Theo stared at her in the faint lights of Paris from the open window. They were still naked in bed. Just moments before they'd been lost in ecstasy.

Now, he felt… He didn't even know how he felt. Except that it wasn't good.

All month they'd been in Paris, he'd felt that same relaxed, joyful sensation he'd had in Santorini, only more so. Was that happiness? He didn't know how else to describe it. Working long days with a team he respected on his dream property deal, and feeling the satisfaction of watching it take shape and knowing, *knowing*, he would finally win, was exhilarating. His work this past month had demanded every bit of his attention. It relaxed him, helping him forget everything he didn't want to remember, shutting up the voices inside him that told him he should have been the one to die.

He'd had his Miss Swenson back. Emmie had been in top form, organizing and collating everything from the geologic survey of the plat site to the percentages of different investors in yen versus euros to the visual impact of the marketing materials.

In spite of her advancing pregnancy, Emmie was tireless, running everything with style, grace and flair. Her new wardrobe, with its tasteful luxury, indicated her as a woman of power in her own right. She was the most incredible second-in-command any CEO could hope for, spending every hour of her day in pursuit of one objective: helping Theo achieve his dreams.

Oh, and at night, she suddenly turned into his wife, the sexiest woman in the world, and set his world on fire.

Happiness. Yes. *Happiness* was the word.

Was it any wonder as the day approached when he'd promised to return with her to live in New York, that Theo might wish they could keep living this wonderful life?

Why would he ever want this to end?

The winning property developer would be expected to remain in Paris to oversee construction, perhaps for years. Theo had people who could do that, but what if he preferred to do it himself? Or what if he wanted to jump into a new, exciting project far from New York? The world was full of empty lots, just waiting for him to build cathedrals of industry, palaces of housing, skyscrapers and shops and parks. The future had no limit.

Especially with Emmie by his side.

So he'd had an idea he'd meant to propose to her tonight: that they'd continue to travel the world securing new property deals, moving from place to place. She'd keep working sixteen-hour days at his side. A nanny could travel with them to take care of their child. Perfect.

But first on the elevator, then later as he sat across from her in candlelight on the Seine, Theo Katrakis, feared in boardrooms and amateur boxing rings, had *chickened out*.

No. Not chickened out, he'd told himself. The time just wasn't yet ripe. Timing was everything.

After making love to her, as Theo held her in his arms, he'd stared at the ceiling, trying to think of the right words to make her want the same life he wanted. No ideas were forthcoming.

He wanted to make his wife happy. He did. But he also didn't want to be trapped in New York, waiting for their son to be born, preparing the nursery and dealing with baby showers and endless intrusions from family and friends. He wanted to build his empire. He wanted to work. Work was life.

And he wanted Emmie with him. At his side. In his office. In his bed.

He cared for her. He wanted her respect. She was the only one who understood him, who saw his flaws and limitations but still accepted him, just as he was. He didn't have to hide with her. He didn't have to pretend.

At least he hadn't—until now.

He forced a smile. "Of course I want to go home."

Still naked in his arms, Emmie looked at him, her heart-shaped lips parted in a breathless dawn of a smile. "So you don't mind—"

"But does New York have to be our only home?" He stroked sweaty tendrils of her blond hair from her cheek. "The world is a big place. We could own it all."

Emmie's lovely face clouded in the shadowy bedroom. "I thought you liked New York. It's your headquarters."

"The company's headquarters, not mine."

"You bought a fifty-million-dollar penthouse to live in."

He shrugged. "An investment, no different from my other properties around the world. Emmie—" he clasped her hand "—we could live anywhere."

She stared at him. "But my family is in New York. Our friends." Her eyes filled with shadow. "I agreed to stay and work in Paris till your project was done. But then you promised we could go home."

"Haven't you been happy, Emmie?" His arms tightened around her, their naked bodies intertwined on the bed in a tangle of sheets. "Don't you enjoy our life here?"

Abruptly, Emmie pulled away. She rose to her feet. He had a single moment to appreciate the sensual curve of her backside in the shadowy light, her honey-blond hair tumbling down her back, before she wrapped herself in a white terrycloth robe from the closet. She turned back, tying the belt.

"I've enjoyed seeing you happy." Meeting his eyes, she added quietly, "Because I'm in love with you, Theo."

Whatever Theo had been about to say was choked off as his throat tightened. Telling himself he'd misheard, he said hoarsely, "What?"

Her violet eyes were huge in the moonlight as she said simply, "I love you."

Turning away, he rose abruptly from the bed, pulling on his robe. He muttered, "You're overtired."

"I'm not, I mean, it's true I am, but that's not why. I'm saying it because it's true. I love you."

It was as if a dam had burst, and once she'd spoken the awful incantation, she couldn't quit repeating it like an evil spell. His mind was whirling. "What does that even mean?"

"I think…*love* means putting the other person ahead of yourself," she said quietly.

His lips twisted downward. "You mean it makes you a slave."

Emmie stared at him from across the luxurious bedroom, with its old oil paintings and marble fireplace full of unlit white candles. Her expression was stricken.

"It's not like that," she protested. Brushing at her eyes, she gave him a small, wistful smile. "Not if both people love each other."

Love each other.

Memory punched through his heart.

His mother's wild, bloodshot eyes. *"I can't leave him. We love each other."*

"He's going to kill you, Mama. And us."

Breaking out in a sweat, Theo turned unsteadily toward the balcony. Strong, he had to be strong. Gripping his hands into fists, he ordered himself to calm the hell down. Cold. He had to be cold.

But it wasn't working.

"I need some fresh air," he gasped and fled.

Outside on the balcony, the night was warm and clear. Clouds covered the stars and all but a sliver of moon. He could see the inky blackness of the Seine below, the shimmer of lights across the river, and beyond it, the soaring Gothic buttresses of Notre Dame on the Île de la Cité.

Emmie silently followed. Beyond the balcony railing, he could see the dark shape of birds against the lowering clouds, hear their melancholy cries as they flew. He took a deep breath.

"I don't want you to love me," he said in a low voice. "I want an alliance of equals. Where we each can live the life we desire, and no one has to sacrifice. No one gets hurt."

"Sorry."

Her shoulders slumped, her lovely face was downcast. And Theo hated himself for disappointing her. Why was she forcing him to hurt her?

He choked out, "You promised you'd never love me."

Emmie looked down at the black river. A beam of moonlight twisted through the clouds, tracing the smooth curve of her cheek. Lifting her head, she said quietly, "And you promised we'd live in New York. To have a home. With friends. Family."

And Theo suddenly knew the life he'd hoped to have with her was impossible. She would never agree to hire a full-time nanny so that she could spend her days working beside him at the office, helping him conquer the world. Emmie would never be parted from her child for the sake of money or power or fame.

Love was what mattered to her. Love he could not give her.

Pain was like a razor blade in his throat as he turned back to the Seine. Moonlight rested the sharp edges of the water's dark waves.

He felt Emmie's gentle hands on his shoulder. "It's all right, Theo. I know you can't love me. I've known it all along. It's my fault. All my fault." She gave him a crooked half smile. "Well, a little bit yours, for being so irresistible."

Even now, she was making jokes, trying to lighten the mood and offer comfort, though he'd hurt her so badly. He tried to smile back. "If I could love anyone—"

"I know." Balling her fists into the pockets of her robe, Emmie took a deep breath. "I'll get over it. Add it to the list of things we'll never discuss again." She turned away. "Forget I said anything."

But as his wife disappeared back into the bedroom, leaving Theo alone on the balcony in the haunted moonlight of Paris, he knew there was no way he'd ever be able to forget.

CHAPTER ELEVEN

How could Emmie have made such a mistake?

How could she have put their baby at risk?

"All right, Mrs. Katrakis." Dr. Hwang's cool eyes focused on hers, as Emmie lay on a towel over the leather sofa on their private jet now on descent into a New York airport. Standing up, the doctor washed her hands in the small galley sink. "You're only three centimeters dilated. We'll get you to the hospital on time."

"Do you—promise?" Emmie panted, as another contraction contorted her body.

"I don't make promises, but it's very likely." The gray-haired doctor glanced at the flight attendant. "You had the pilot relay the emergency?"

"An ambulance will be waiting when we land," the young woman replied, looking relieved that Emmie wasn't going to give birth on the plane.

Emmie couldn't blame her. She could hardly believe they'd cut it so close.

Her due date was still a week away, and everyone said first babies always arrived late. Emmie had thought she'd have plenty of time to set up the penthouse nursery before she went into labor, upon which she'd serenely grab a prepared overnight bag and Theo would escort her to the

Manhattan hospital they'd chosen. She'd get an epidural for the pain, the labor would be hard but endurable, then afterward she'd introduce her baby to family and friends in a comfortable, spacious hospital room filled with flowers.

But Pierre Harcourt had strung them along until that very morning, when after three weeks of asking several developers for modifications and revisions of their bids, he'd finally signed a binding contract with Katrakis Enterprises. Theo had been right. They'd won. But she'd been right, too. It had all taken longer than they'd hoped.

To be fair, Theo had told her more than once that she should return to New York without him. But she hadn't. Even that morning, as they'd been packing for the plane, he'd asked her if it wouldn't be better for them to just stay in Paris until the baby was born. She'd shot down that idea, too.

She'd wanted to prove their marriage could still work. That she could love him and he could totally not love her but they could still succeed together as a couple. As a family.

And this was the result.

"We'll make it to the hospital," Emmie said, forcing her cheeks into a cheerful smile. "That's a relief, isn't it?"

"A relief," Theo agreed, but his handsome face was pale beneath his tan. Going to the galley, he returned with a bottle of cool water and handed it to her as she smoothed her sundress back over her knees, sitting up on the leather sofa.

"Thanks." She drank the water in gulps. "It'll be a funny story to tell our son someday. That we went into labor halfway over the Atlantic."

"Funny," he said, but he didn't meet her eyes.

An ambulance was waiting on the tarmac when they landed at Teterboro thirty minutes later. Emmie was whisked off the plane on a stretcher and placed in the back of the ambulance as the concierge doctor spoke quietly to the paramedics, handing over care.

"Come with me," Emmie called to Theo, who was lingering behind, his shoulders hunched, his handsome face stricken.

"Not enough room. He'll have to follow us, ma'am," one of the paramedics said and closed the ambulance door.

By the time Emmie arrived at the Midtown hospital, the one closest to their house and where she'd planned to give birth, her body was racked with increasing pain. She'd turned in the paperwork weeks before, so was quickly wheeled to a private room in the maternity ward on the tenth floor. By then, the contractions were so bad she couldn't breathe. She nearly threw up from the pain.

"Epidural," she croaked when she saw her obstetrician in the door.

After checking her, the doctor shook her head. "Sorry, Mrs. Katrakis." Nurses came closer, putting monitoring equipment on her belly to check the baby's heart, and on Emmie's finger to check her oxygen levels. "It's far too late for that. You're at nine centimeters. It's almost time to push."

"No—it can't be already—" Emmie couldn't go into labor now, not yet. Not without her husband.

Where was he?

Even without the flashing lights and siren of a speeding ambulance, the drive from Teterboro should have taken forty-five minutes, an hour in bad traffic. Where was he?

"Now, Mrs. Katrakis," her obstetrician said and positioned herself between her knees, "push!"

Emmie gasped for breath and cried and retched, and she pushed. She pushed most of all, bearing down with all her strength, until she thought she might pass out or die and wasn't even sure that would be a bad thing—except her baby…her baby had to live.

When it was finally over, she took a full gasping breath as the doctor turned away with the precious bundle. Emmie craned her head around the doctor, but she couldn't see her baby. Why was it so quiet? What was happening?

"My baby… Why isn't he crying? What's wrong?" She turned, sweaty and crying. "Theo."

But it wasn't her husband she'd heard coming through the door, just a nurse to begin the afterbirth protocols. Emmie turned back to the doctor.

"Give me my baby. Now or I'll…"

A sudden small cry, weak at first, then louder and heartier. The obstetrician turned back toward her, holding a tiny baby wrapped in a clean towel.

"Mrs. Katrakis," she said gently, "I'd like you to meet your son."

The tiny newborn was placed in Emmie's arms, against her bare skin, and she felt a rush of joy she'd never known. The baby blinked in confusion, yawning, looking up at her sleepily with dark eyes. But as their eyes met, Emmie felt a strange recognition. Her son. Hers.

She caressed the baby's cheek, marveling. "And he's all right? He's okay?"

"He took a minute to decide to breathe, but yes. He's fine. Seven pounds, six ounces. A healthy baby boy."

"Thank you, Dr. Sanchez." Her son was born. And he was healthy. He was fine.

But Emmie had given birth alone. Her husband had never arrived. He'd missed the whole thing.

The kindly nurse helped Emmie wash up, helping her into a clean hospital gown. As she was checked by the obstetrician, a different nurse washed her baby, before he was placed back in Emmie's arms.

For long moments, as nurses and doctors buzzed around them in the room, Emmie just sat in the bed holding her baby, wondering at his beauty, touching his skin, holding him close. When he started to whimper, with the nurse's encouragement Emmie tentatively placed her baby to her breast. As he instinctively started to suckle, she watched his tiny face turn blissful and felt relief that was like joy.

But where was Theo?

The sun started to lower behind Manhattan's skyscrapers, and she grew increasingly worried. Had he been in an accident? Was he hurt, dying, his car smashed up on the I-95 freeway?

When the baby slept, she called his phone.

There was no answer. She left a message, then another.

Finally, she phoned Honora, her father, and her brothers, to tell them her baby news. Honora was elated and promised to come at once. Her father and brothers, busy with a big emergency plumbing job, shouted with joy. They promised to come in the morning.

She checked the news anxiously, but there was no mention of a massive pileup on the highway. She left Theo more messages. She received her dinner delivered on a tray and was thinking about calling the police when Honora appeared in the door with her oldest child.

As Emmie's best friend oohed and aahed over Emmie's new baby, Honora's three-year-old, Kara, was less impressed.

"I already have one," the little girl archly informed Emmie, as if to warn her against trying to pawn off the baby on Kara's family. Emmie laughed, but it was strained in her growing anxiety. Where was Theo? Why wasn't he here?

"Adorable." Honora sat on the edge of the bed, glowing but still slender, just recently pregnant herself with her third child. "What are you going to name him? Did you decide?"

"We haven't had a chance…" For all his determination to marry her and secure his heir, Theo never seemed comfortable talking about their baby's future. When Emmie had suggested possible names, he'd always said there was no rush, then changed the subject.

"Really? After two long months of marriage?" Honora said teasingly, then looked around the hospital room. "Where is Theo, anyway? Did he sneak off for some personal time with his laptop? Off making a super-important phone call?"

Licking her cracked lips, Emmie said slowly, "I… I don't know."

Her friend frowned. "What do you mean?"

"He was supposed to follow my ambulance in his car. But I haven't…" She covered her eyes with her hand, overwhelmed. "That was hours ago. He's not answering his phone. I'm scared he was in an accident."

"Oh, Emmie," Honora said softly. She patted her shoulder. "Don't worry. I'm sure there's a good explanation." She gave a rueful laugh. "If you only knew half of what Nico put me through back in the day…" Whipping out her phone, she placed a call. "Hey, babe," she said cheerfully. "Can you do me a favor?"

Theo was in hell.

From the moment they'd left Paris, he'd felt a rising sense of dread making his body tense and belly churn for reasons he didn't understand.

After all, he'd won the Harcourt prize, just as he'd hoped. Pierre Harcourt had accepted his final bid, and Celine had even congratulated him with kind words, "The best man won," before rushing out of the boardroom to meet up with her new boyfriend.

Assuming the legal paperwork went smoothly, Theo expected to break ground soon. If everything went according to schedule, his new Paris development—a gorgeous mix of retail, office and housing surrounded by dramatic, environmentally friendly gardens—would be finished in two years. It was thrilling.

And yet he'd left it all behind. Abandoned the project at the starting gate. For Emmie.

He'd promised his wife they could live in Manhattan. It was the least he could do. A consolation prize he could give her, he thought bitterly, in lieu of loving her.

Emmie and his son deserved better.

"I'm in love with you, Theo."

Remembering her luminous face as she'd spoken those words still made him feel sick inside.

How long would it be before Emmie realized that Theo, with his cold heart, wasn't good enough for her? Before his son realized it, too?

He'd sent her to the hospital alone. Because he was scared. Because he couldn't bear to see her pain. If that didn't make her love evaporate, nothing would.

He swallowed hard. The truth was, all he could offer anyone was wealth and a job in real-estate development—neither of which Emmie cared about. He'd offered her palaces and gold, when what she wanted, what she *needed*, was his love…

Standing in the grass, Theo leaned his head against the fence, feeling the hard surface against his clammy forehead. Exhaling, he lifted his gaze and looked out at Manhattan's skyline across the Hudson. As sunset fell behind him, the last red rays shimmered over the gleaming steel and glass skyscrapers across the dark river.

When Emmie had gone into labor on the plane halfway over the Atlantic—too late to return to Paris—he'd wanted to flee, to cover his eyes and run. But there was no escaping a plane, not unless one wanted to jump out at twenty thousand feet. Seeing his wife's pain, he'd been overwhelmed with panic and fear. What if he lost Emmie? What if they lost their baby? It would be his fault, for keeping them in Paris so long. Theo had paced in agony, even as he'd tried to look strong and reassuring. But he'd never felt so useless, so helpless, not since—

Not since—

Was Emmie still in labor? Had his son already been born?

Theo had meant to follow her to the hospital, honest to God. But as he'd collapsed into the sports car waiting for him at the airport, he hadn't even driven the short distance to the Lincoln Tunnel before his vision closed in, creating a tunnel all its own.

So he'd veered off into a small park in Weehawken overlooking the river. Parking the car in the half-empty lot, he'd leaned his head against the steering wheel, feeling like he was going to die.

"Theo, what have you done?" The shriek of his mother's voice over the crackle of the fire. *"You've killed him!"*

Pushing the memory away, Theo had stumbled out of the car into the small park, trying to catch his breath.

The August evening was sticky and hot. Leaning against the fence on the edge of the river, he could almost see his breath in the thick humid air, puffs of smoke like the ghosts of those he'd lost. The father he'd never known. The emotionally distant uncle who'd given him a home.

His mother. His stepfather.

Your fault, a dark voice whispered. *You killed them both.*

Now, Theo stared across the water, watching the shimmering glass skyscrapers on the horizon turn orange, then red, then finally violet, as the sun set slowly behind him.

It would be easy, he thought, just to drive back to the airport, and disappear—to Singapore or Dubai or anywhere. People might despise him for abandoning his wife and son.

Only Theo would know the truth: they'd be better-off without him.

Emmie was good and pure, his baby son an innocent soul. What happiness could a man like Theo possibly bring them? What could he do except cause them pain?

"There you are."

Turning, Theo was astonished to see Nico Ferraro crossing the grass. He almost rubbed his eyes, just to be sure Nico, too, wasn't a ghost. His friend smiled.

"My wife called. Said you were having a little trouble finding your way to the hospital." Glancing back, he looked at Theo's parked Maserati with the door still hanging open. "Car trouble?"

"How did you find me—" Then he remembered how last year, after his Lamborghini was stolen, he'd angrily told Nico he was going to put a GPS tracker in every car. His company's head of security would be able to monitor his cars' locations, under strict orders never to share the information with any woman, be she secretary, girlfriend, or wife who might invade Theo's privacy. Emmie had no idea.

"Right," Nico said, nodding with a grin. "I convinced Carter you might be in danger. He's right over there, in fact, with a couple guys just in case." He waved vaguely toward a black van on the far edge of the parking lot. Theo's head of security nodded in return. "So," Nico turned back, "what the hell are you doing here?"

"Nothing much," Theo said tightly.

Snorting, Nico gestured to the van, and his head of security drove away. His friend faced Theo with a sigh. "So you're just hanging out in a park. While your wife just went through labor alone and is now worried your mangled body is going to appear in the morgue. Which made *my* wife send me all over town looking for you, then drive to Jersey in traffic. Thanks for that, by the way." He tilted his head. "What's really going on?"

"I told you. Nothing."

"Uh-huh." Nico looked him over, then shook his head with a low laugh. "Look, I get it. I've been there. But my wife asked me to find you. So you have two choices. Either you phone Emmie and explain the truth about your little park excursion or…"

"Or?"

Nico's dark eyes met his. "Or you come to the hospital with me right now. And I'll explain about your car trouble."

Theo felt trapped in a corner. His hands tightened, and for a moment, he actually considered a third option: punching his way out. Then he looked at his friend's sympathetic but firm expression.

"Fine," he growled.

So Nico drove him to the hospital, arranging for an employee to pick up the Maserati. Walking through the hospital's revolving door, Theo felt numb. He followed Nico onto the tenth floor, past the nurses' desk.

"It's a little late for visiting," a nurse objected as they walked past.

"Not at all. He's the happy father of room 1035," Nico said, pushing him forward.

Theo felt like he was walking through water, or in a nightmare blurry as a Renoir painting, as they rounded the corner into Emmie's room. He saw Honora trying to entertain her toddler with a coloring book. Vases of colorful flowers beneath the hospital's fluorescent light.

Outside, the night was now dark. The window's glass reflected the image of an exhausted woman in the bed smiling down beatifically at the baby in her arms. And Theo saw himself, a dark-haired man standing at a distance like a stranger.

"Look what I found," Nico said, and both women turned to them with a sob of relief.

"Uncle Theo!" little Kara cried, flinging herself around his legs. He looked down at her.

"Hello, sugarplum."

"Theo." Emmie wiped her eyes with a visibly shaking hand. "I was afraid something terrible had happened."

It had, Theo thought. Long, long ago. And it meant he could never be the man she wanted him to be. With a deep breath, he forced himself to smile. "Here I am."

"But where have you been? I left so many messages—"

"Car trouble," Nico said succinctly. "His engine stopped."

It was technically true.

"Uncle Theo, look at my drawing! Look!" Three-year-old Kara waggled her page covered with squiggles.

"It's…nice," he said, unable to manage his usual charm that had made him a favorite with the toddler. His eyes met Emmie's, and suddenly his heart was in his throat.

"We should go," Nico said.

"It's past Kara's bedtime." Meeting her husband's eyes, Honora quickly gathered up her daughter's crayons. "Granddad will be wondering where we are."

"And so will his wife, since she's been watching him and the baby." Nico scooped up Kara, ignoring her protests. The family abruptly disappeared, leaving Theo alone with his wife and newborn son in the hospital room.

Emmie looked at him.

"You missed everything," she said, her voice strained.

"I'm sorry."

"Well." Her expression relented. "You're here now. Come meet your son."

His throat was tight as he inched forward to Emmie and the baby cuddled together. "He's healthy? You're both all right?"

"Fine. Come see him." Looking at the sleeping baby dreamily, she patted the side of her hospital bed.

Awkwardly, he sat down on the very edge. His gaze fell on some flowers on her nightstand, with a visible card.

You're a brave lady. Best of luck with him.
Carlos Mondragón

Looking around at all the flowers filling the hospital room, in red, purple, yellow, pink and blue, blue most of all, it struck Theo how long he'd been missing. Long enough for Emmie to give birth and his acquaintances to hear about it. Long enough for them to *send flowers*.

Theo really was a selfish bastard. He looked down at his rough, dry hands and repeated helplessly, "I'm sorry."

"No, stop. It's not your fault you had car trouble." But there was something stiff in her voice, as if she didn't believe her own words. As the baby woke and started to fuss, Emmie forced a smile. "Come hold him."

Theo looked nervously at the unhappy baby. "I don't know if…"

"Take off your shirt."

"What?"

"Just do it." Reluctantly, he obeyed, dropping it to the linoleum floor. She lifted her free hand. "Now hold your arms like this."

Jaw tight, he held out his arms. His wife gently lifted the squirming infant, who wore only a diaper, against Theo's bare chest.

Cuddled against his father, skin to skin, the baby gave a little hiccup, then soothed by the rise and fall of Theo's breath, his eyelids grew heavy. His tiny body relaxed back into sleep.

"Good job," she said softly. "Isn't he beautiful?"

Theo looked down at his newborn son. An innocent child who'd depend on him for everything. Not just for his home and education but to show him the meaning of a good life. To teach him how to be a man.

Theo felt something twist his heart, squeezing until it pulled the blood from his veins, choking oxygen from his brain.

Leaning over the bed, Emmie wrapped her arm around Theo's shoulders and looked down at the baby dreamily. "What should we name him?" She gave a light laugh. "Theo Junior?"

He sucked in his breath. Wrap Theo's name, with all its horrifying baggage, around their baby's neck like an anchor?

"Call him what you want," Theo said tightly. "Just don't name him after me."

She turned, clearly mystified. "Why?"

Theo looked into her violet eyes and suddenly knew she needed a better man than he could be. If he stayed, if he was true to his vows, then not just his son but his wife, too, would be sucked dry, giving him love he didn't deserve. They'd give him everything and finally drown beneath the weight of Theo's dark, unredeemable soul.

"I didn't have car trouble." He took a deep breath and told her the truth. "I just didn't want to be here."

CHAPTER TWELVE

DURING THE HOURS her husband had been missing, Emmie had been tortured by thoughts of a car accident, a heart attack, a violent mugging—all the tragedies of life that could happen at any time.

When Theo had appeared in the doorway, her fear had melted away. He was safe. She told herself she'd been foolish to worry.

But looking at his guilty, haunted face, she'd felt a flash of something she didn't want to admit, even to herself. Something dark.

Now she knew what it was. She loved him. She'd somehow thought, if she sacrificed her needs for his, if she was a perfect wife and gave him everything she had, he might someday love her back. Now she knew she'd been lying to herself.

"I want an alliance of equals," he'd told her in Paris. "Where we each can live the life we desire, and no one has to sacrifice. No one gets hurt."

There was no such alliance. Emmie had sacrificed in Paris, working for months on a project she didn't care about, when she'd wanted to be home getting ready for their baby. And Theo had sacrificed, too, leaving his Paris dream project barely started and returning to New York, a place he clearly didn't want to be.

Theo didn't want her life. She didn't want his.

But still, in spite of everything, some part of Emmie had hoped desperately that they could find a way to be happy together. That somehow, either she would stop loving him—or he'd start loving her...

Now, all those hopes came crashing down.

"You didn't want to be here?" she choked out.

Theo looked down at their sleeping baby in his powerful arms. Holding their newborn against his bare, hard-muscled chest, he was the picture of sexy masculinity.

Except he lacked the joyful face of a new father. For the first time, Emmie noticed the hollows beneath his dark eyes. He had the expression of a man trapped in his worst nightmare. He didn't answer.

"You...don't want our son?" she whispered. Waves of grief and hurt slammed into her.

His black eyes glittered. "He deserves better."

"You're his father. And my husband. Who better to—"

"Someone. Anyone." Standing up, he carefully placed their sleeping baby back in her lap. He took a step back from her bed. "I'm sorry."

Blinking back tears, she tried to breathe, to find her sympathy and compassion. But she couldn't. He wasn't just rejecting her. He was rejecting their son. "No."

"I'm no good, Emmie. I've tried. But the truth is I can never be the man you want. The man he needs."

As he picked his shirt up off the floor and put it back on, she stared at him in the dark quiet of the hospital room.

"You're leaving us," she breathed.

Now that it had finally happened, she realized she'd always known this was how it would end. She would love him; he would leave her. And yet part of her still couldn't believe it. "But you're the one who wanted us to be a family. I was marrying someone else! You interrupted my wedding and wouldn't take no for an answer!"

Head bowed, Theo stood silently next to the bed, hands in his trouser pockets, black shirt only half-buttoned. His hard face was shadowed by the lamplight. "I know."

"Just because I said I loved you?" she cried. The baby woke and started to whimper. She felt like whimpering, too.

Theo took a breath, started to say something, then just shook his head. "It's more than that."

"Then, why? Tell me why!"

Theo's eyes were bleak. "What do I know about being a father?" He turned toward his distorted reflection in the window. "My father died when I was a few months old. My mother told me he overdosed on pills, trying to sleep over my crying."

Emmie sucked in her breath. "She *told* you that?"

His lips curled. "She was trying to explain why being a parent was so hard. Love was hard for her, too. There was a parade of men through my childhood. She shared drugs with them and fell madly in love." His voice held no emotion. "There was a different man every few months, some of whom she married, none of them very good, often stoned or drunk or stealing her money. And then..."

"Then?"

His dark eyes shadowed. "When I was ten, she met Panos Papadopolous. He was older, and rich. She said she'd met her soulmate who'd take care of her forever. He proposed to her the night they met, and we moved to his ancestral home on Lyra. My mother returned from the honeymoon with two things—a black eye and my sister in her belly."

"What happened?"

He shrugged, twisting the gold band on his left hand. "They fell into a pattern. He'd get mad and smack her around. They'd do drugs together, and he'd graciously forgive her. After Sofia was born, it was worse. Whenever he felt upset about his failing business, or someone disrespected him, or he was worried about his dwindling family fortune, he dealt with it by beating my mother. Just because he could." Looking down, he said in a low voice, "That's what love means to me. Either kicking someone when they're down. Or being the victim on the ground."

Emmie's heart was pounding. Her family life had been chaotic and stressful sometimes, with five children, a sick mother and bills not always paid. But never abusive. Never that. She'd always known her family loved her. "It's horrible. How did you get out?"

"When I tried to protect my mother, he'd beat me, too. Until I became taller than he was. One day, when he punched me, I punched back. We nearly killed each other. I begged my mother to grab my sister and leave, but she wouldn't. She said she couldn't survive on the street with two children and no husband. So she sent me off to a boarding school in England. A school for problem boys. Not to protect me." His lip twisted in a sneer. "To protect *him*."

"Theo…" she breathed, agonized.

He paced across the hospital room's linoleum floor, looking back blindly at the dark window faintly smeared with the lights of Midtown Manhattan.

"I came home from school the summer I was fifteen and found my mother in the hospital with two black eyes and a purple bruise around her neck. He'd gotten notice from the bank that they were foreclosing on the house, so he'd decided to strangle her. And I saw Sofia…" He closed his eyes.

She felt a chill. "What?"

"With me away at school and my mother in the hospital, Sofia was the only one left for him to hurt. I found her hiding in her bedroom closet. He'd wanted money for drugs so he'd demanded her gold locket. Sofia loved that locket. She hugged it whenever our mother was gone because it had her picture inside it. But Panos screamed threats about beating her black and blue and ripped it out of her hand. She was quivering, hiding from him in the dark. She was five years old."

"Oh, no…" Emmie looked down at her sleeping baby and wondered how any parent could hurt their own child.

Theo set his jaw. "Panos had left to find his supplier, so I took Sofia to stay with neighbors in the village. When I returned, I found him high as a kite, smoking and frying honey fritters on the stove. I told him I was taking my mother and sister away for good and if he tried to follow us, I'd kill him."

"What did he do?"

"He screamed insults and threats. When I didn't back down, he picked up the pan of burning oil and threw it at me. I ducked." He glanced down toward his ankle. "Mostly."

"Your scar," she breathed. "It didn't come from an engine fire in a car race."

"No." He gave a grim smile. "I dodged the pan then punched him in the mouth. His cigarette fell into the spilled cooking oil and started to burn. Panos grabbed a kitchen knife and lunged at me. But he slipped and fell. Either the fall knocked him out or the drugs did. I don't know. But when I tried to lift him, to drag him out, I couldn't. He was twice my weight—"

"You tried to save him?" Emmie said, astounded.

He shook his head. "The kitchen filled with smoke, and

I could feel the heat burning my skin. I couldn't budge him off the floor. So I turned and ran. I left him to die, Emmie."

"Good. The man got what he deserved," she replied vengefully. He blinked at her vehemence. Looking down at her own baby, who'd fallen back to sleep, she said, "You have nothing to feel guilty about."

His jaw was tight as he looked down at his hands. "Don't I?"

"It's over now, Theo," she tried again. "It's all over."

He looked up at her bleakly.

"It'll never be over," he whispered.

Theo wanted to flee the hospital and run twenty miles, to punch a bag until he collapsed, to start a fight with someone who'd knock him bloody. Anything rather than face the tenderness and pity and love he saw shining from his wife's face.

His hands clenched at his sides. "The fire was already climbing the walls when I left him. I ran onto the beach and watched the red and orange flames consume the house, crackling and spiraling embers up into the night. As the house burned, I felt *glad*. I thought we were free. Then I heard my mother behind me."

Emmie's lovely face was wan as she listened. He had to tell her the worst. She had to know. His throat was tight.

"Mama was still in her hospital gown and covered with purple bruises, but she'd worried about him, now I was back. She'd come to save him. From me." He still remembered her agonizing shriek.

"Where is he? Theo, what have you done? You've killed him!"

Emmie took a deep breath, her violet eyes luminous with sympathy.

He closed his eyes, not wanting to remember. "She screamed his name and tried to run into the house. When I stopped her, she slapped me in the face, clawing at my eyes, kicking me till I backed away. 'I love him!' she kept screaming. She ran into the house. She was barely inside before it collapsed, exploding into fire."

Theo's knees felt weak, as if he were still that boy again.

Emmie sucked in her breath. Then, still sitting on the bed with their baby, she reached out her hand.

"It wasn't your fault," she whispered. She held out her hand to where he stood alone in the hospital room. "You were fifteen. You did everything you could to protect her. She made her choice."

He didn't move. "Because she loved him."

Dropping her hand, Emmie looked startled. "That's not love."

"Love means putting someone else's needs ahead of your own. Isn't that what you said?"

"Yes, but—"

"The police ruled the fire an accident. But they'd often come to the house after he'd beaten her. She'd always refused to press charges, so I think they felt bad for us. For Sofia, at least."

"And you. You were just a child, too."

"Yeah." His lips curved sardonically. "Well. A neighbor was willing to adopt Sofia. But no one wanted an angry fifteen-year-old. I couldn't go back to boarding school. There was no money. I ran away from a state orphanage and lived on the streets of Athens for a while. I thought I was tough, until a bunch of older boys beat me into a bloody pile on the street because they thought I'd stolen their food. Which I hadn't." Rubbing the back of his mussed hair, he gave her a wry grin. "Though, I'd wanted to."

Theo looked across the hospital room at his sweetly sleeping baby boy. "The funny thing was, they did me a favor. A social worker found me at the hospital and told me my uncle from America had been looking for me."

"See?" Emmie said warmly. "That's another example of love—"

"My uncle was lonely. His wife had just left him. He wanted a companion who wouldn't leave. I started learning his business, property development. My uncle was kind, in his way. But weak."

"Weak, how?"

Theo thought of his Uncle Andrew's face as he'd taken him to his small, shabby office in Upstate New York.

"I'll teach you how to pitch. Work is the thing that can save us. That will never leave you. It's cold and logical. Live to work, and no one can ever hurt you."

And Theo had learned that well. He'd thrown himself into business like an anchor into a bottomless ocean. Over the last twenty years, he'd turned his uncle's small business into a global empire.

He sighed. "Even after his ex-wife married another man, Uncle Andrew never got over it. When he was sad, he'd drive by her house. When he was drunk, he'd look her up online. Other than that, he'd work, but he didn't even do that very well, since he was distracted by his yearning for her, like a missing piece of his body." His jaw tightened as he looked at Emmie. "That's what love does to you."

She looked away. "You're right. Love is awful. But also," she said and lifted her gaze, her lovely face filled with emotion, "it's the only thing that makes life worth living."

Theo staggered back a step, looking at the light and love shining in her eyes.

"I wish I could love you," he whispered. He shook his head hollowly. "My life has burned my heart out of me."

"But you told me everything—didn't you?" At his trembling nod, she gave him a slow-rising smile. "There are no more secrets between us. Now you've trusted me that much, maybe things can be different. We can be different."

"I don't want you to be different, Emmie. You're sweet and good. I won't have you throwing your love away on someone without a heart. I'm not going to drag you down." His gaze fell to their son. He said softly, "Or him." He turned away. "Good-bye."

"Theo!"

At the agony in her voice, he froze. He closed his eyes. He couldn't look back and see her imploring face. If he did, he knew he'd never have the strength to leave. But he had to. For Emmie. For his son. He pressed his fingertips against his eyes.

"Forget the prenup," he whispered. "You can have anything you want. Money, cars, houses. Just take it. Everything I have is yours—"

His voice caught, and he fled the room. He didn't look back. Stumbling down the hall, he couldn't wait for the elevator so ran down ten flights of stairs. At the ground floor, he knocked the exit door against the wall in his desperation to escape. Staggering into the street, he hailed a yellow cab, feeling like he was going to die.

Knowing that the best part of him just had.

CHAPTER THIRTEEN

THEO STARED DOWN at the divorce papers that had just been delivered overnight to his Paris office. Along with Emmie's diamond engagement ring.

Emmie hadn't gotten a high-powered attorney to fight for her rights, as she should have done. These papers looked like something she'd printed off the internet. She didn't ask for the penthouse or any other residence. She wanted no alimony, not even the million dollars the prenup had entitled her to. She asked only for two things: child support, which he was already legally required to pay. And the used minivan he'd bought on impulse in Queens.

Closing his eyes, he exhaled. It was so Emmie. She wouldn't protect herself, so he'd do it for her. He'd tell his own shark of a lawyer to give her more than she'd asked for. Far, far more.

It had been two months since he'd left her in the hospital, and though he'd immediately returned to Paris and tried to bury himself in work, he still felt her absence, every second, every moment. For the first few days after he'd abandoned her, she'd tried to call and left messages. Then she'd abruptly stopped. Emmie finally must have accepted what they both knew to be true.

But he hoped she was happy. God, how he prayed she

was, her and his son. He'd almost reached out to Wilson, the penthouse's butler, just to confirm Emmie and the baby were all right. But he hadn't. He was barely holding on as it was. He had to make a clean break.

Theo was looking at that clean break right now. Holding it in his hands. All he had to do was forward the divorce papers to his lawyer in New York to get the ball rolling.

Divorce. It was what Theo had wanted. Wasn't it? So why didn't he feel at peace? Why did he feel like punching the wall?

"Stop—wait—you can't go in there," his elderly secretary protested in French.

"Try and stop me," came the pert response in the same language, and suddenly the door to his private office was flung open, and his sister strode in. Sofia's eyes lit up when she saw him. "Thank heaven I caught you. I need you to take my present with you."

What was she talking about? He stared at her as his secretary came in, clearly discomfited.

"I'm sorry, *monsieur*, she—"

"It's all right, Gertrude." Theo gestured for his secretary to close the door. After she left, he lifted an eyebrow at Sofia. "You couldn't call first?"

"I tried that. You always ignore my calls when you're at work."

Through the window, he could see the gray rain over Paris, the eternal traffic around the Arc de Triomphe. "I call you back eventually."

"You take too long." With a tsk, Sofia sat down in the hard chair across his desk. "And even then, you're too busy to talk. Sensible people go out to dinner with friends and enjoy life. You just work, exercise and sleep!"

"That is how I enjoy *my* life." But even as Theo spoke

those words, he knew he was lying. He couldn't remember the last time he'd enjoyed anything. Even Paris's famous cuisine tasted like ash in his mouth.

"Nobody could enjoy the life you live. Spending two months away from your wife and child! It's lucky for you I'm here to make sure you're not utterly miserable." His little sister smiled at him, and for a moment he almost smiled back.

He'd never intended to have a regular relationship with Sofia. But since she'd returned to Paris last month, after a summer traveling the world, she'd absolutely refused to take his hints that he'd prefer to be left alone. No. She showed up at his hotel room and suggested a stroll through the Jardin du Luxembourg. She'd twice phoned him in a panic, once claiming her date had abandoned her and later that her purse had been stolen, and when he arrived in a rush, he'd found her smiling like a cat with a canary feather hanging from its mouth, standing in front of a chic restaurant, where she'd gotten them reservations. "It's the only way you'd come," she explained. As if that excused it!

For the last two months, no matter how hard Theo tried to push her away, Sofia had persisted.

"That's love."

He heard the words as if Emmie had spoken them in his ear.

Theo sucked in his breath. No. He couldn't let himself think that way. Not now. Not after everything he'd done—

"So, what do you want?" he demanded now.

"Not much, big brother." Sofia sat back in her chair serenely. "Just a small favor. Very small."

She'd really changed since they'd left Lyra, he thought. The young woman looking at him now, in her red lipstick and chic little suit, had deep self-confidence and a determined glint in her eye. She'd come into her own. But no wonder, when... He did mental arithmetic. He was almost forty. That meant Sofia was almost thirty.

How the hell did that happen?

"What favor?" he growled.

"It's nothing." She placed a small blue box on his desk. "Just this."

Theo stared down at the wrapped present with its big blue bow. "What the hell is that?"

Sofia sighed. "I got your wife's invitation. I meant to RSVP weeks ago but then got caught up with my new job at the museum. Also, I've been seeing someone, and..." She snorted. "Why am I explaining? You understand. You always wait till the last minute. I was counting on it when I came here."

"Emmie invited you to a party?" Theo was bewildered.

She rolled her eyes. "I felt bad about ignoring her when we were in Lyra, so I decided to blow her away at the shower." Smiling down proudly at her wrapped gift, she confided, "They're little blue baby booties I knitted myself." Lifting a manicured hand high in the air, she pretended to do a mic drop. "Now, *that's* how you make amends. But I didn't finish making them till last night, and by then, even the fastest shipping wouldn't make it in time. Then I remembered you were still in Paris. I must say, sometimes it's nice to have a workaholic brother with his own plane." She grinned, rising to her feet. "Thanks, big brother. I really appreciate this."

"She's having a baby shower." He'd gotten that much.

"Yes." Frowning at him, she spoke with exaggerated slowness, as if explaining something simple to someone not so bright. "And I need you to bring it with you when you fly to New York today. For the party tonight."

His throat suddenly hurt. "Sorry. I'm not going."

"Of course you're going. The invitation said coed. I assumed you were the reason. Emmie wanted you to be there." Her brow furrowed. "Are you really not going?"

Theo felt a hard twist in his chest. He cleared his throat. "I'm too busy to leave Paris at the moment." To prove it, he moved the cursor vaguely around his computer screen. "We're about to break ground on our project. The biggest in central Paris in decades. That doesn't leave much time to loll around eating cake with friends."

Sofia looked at him pityingly. "I see."

And that was just it. He was afraid she did see.

Theo rose to his feet. "I'm sorry I can't take your gift personally, but my secretary will arrange it to be sent in time by express courier. Where's the party?"

"A friend of hers is hosting. Some beach house in the Hamptons."

Beach house. That meant Honora and Nico. His closest friends, other than Emmie. He felt a razor blade in his throat.

Pushing papers around his desk, he said hoarsely, "Thanks for coming by, but I have a lot of work to do…"

Sofia didn't move. She was staring at those papers. *"Theo."*

He followed her gaze to Emmie's diamond ring resting on the divorce papers.

"Emmie's leaving you?" Sofia breathed. She looked up. "What happened?"

He set his jaw, looking away. "I don't want to talk about it."

"You can't have broken up. Why?"

Turning from his desk, Theo went to the large arched window and looked out at the gray drizzle of Paris. Leaning his arm against the glass, he looked down at the busy lanes of traffic swarming around the Arc de Triomphe. Swallowing hard, he forced himself to say, "Emmie and I realized we weren't suited for marriage. It was a mutual decision."

"No way." His sister's voice was incredulous. "The woman I met in Lyra was totally in love with you."

Theo set his jaw. For a moment, he thought of ordering her out.

But this was his little sister. Was he really going to shut her out of his life? Now, after everything?

He'd lost Emmie, who'd been his best friend, first as his secretary, then as his wife. He figured he'd lost Nico and Honora, too. He didn't want to hear their criticism, so he hadn't returned their messages. He'd left them as gifts to Emmie, along with his penthouse, his cars, his fortune.

And his son. He suddenly realized he didn't even know the boy's name. The only way he'd survived the last two months was by avoiding knowing.

Cold. He had to stay cold.

But as he folded his arms, he was suddenly sweating in his tailored suit. "She's better-off without me. You know what I am."

"What are you?"

Theo stared at her bleakly.

"A murderer," he whispered.

Sofia came forward, her eyes wide. "No."

"She died because of me."

"Mama made her choice. You tried to save her, you *tried*. But she chose him over us. Over and over."

"I should have found a way." His voice caught. As he sank into his desk chair, his eyes were stinging.

His sister put her hand on his shoulder. "You were only fifteen, and you saved us—both of us. Because of you, I had a good life. You sacrificed everything for me," she said quietly. "Don't you remember?"

"No." The emotions he'd repressed for decades seemed to be whirling around him, making him dizzy. He felt like he couldn't breathe. He yanked off his silk tie.

"After Mama died, Mrs. Samaras wanted to take me in. But I wouldn't go there without you. I clung to you. The social worker was going to send both of us to the orphanage instead. Then you took me aside and said I had to go with nice Mrs. Samaras. You said I'd be warm and loved with plenty to eat. You told me you had somewhere wonderful to live, too. It was only later I realized you were lying. You were alone."

Theo stared at her. In the brutal aftermath of the fire, he'd wanted to cling to his baby sister, too. She'd been his only family left. But he'd known Sofia would have a better life if she was adopted by Eleni Samaras, a childless widow who baked fresh bread in her tidy kitchen and had a garden full of flowers and chickens.

He closed his eyes. "You were young, innocent. The fire wasn't your fault."

"It wasn't yours, either. You still ended up starving on the street." Her hand covered his. "You've watched out for me your whole life. Protecting me from my father. Finding me a home. Sending me to college. Even letting me butt in, when you returned to Lyra and wanted to demolish the house alone. You've always put me first." She took a deep breath. "Mama taught us all the wrong things about love. But Theo…you showed me what the best of love could be."

Theo stared at her, shocked into silence.

His sister smiled. "It's why I'm taking you to dinner next week. To tell you about the man I've met." She blushed.

"It's getting serious. He's going to ask me to marry him. And I'm going to say *yes*."

"Sofia…"

She grinned. "So expect a phone call from me soon, with me in a fluster about my Fiat getting a flat tire. Right in front of a very nice two-star tavern in the *Septième*." Her smile faded, even as her eyes shone in the gray light of the Paris office. "Because I finally found a man who can live up to my brother. The kindest, strongest, most loving man in the world. A man who protects those he loves. At any cost."

Theo's heart was pounding. The way his sister described him was so different than how he saw himself. Not a monster? A hero?

He was the one who'd taught Sofia how to love?

"Love means putting the other person ahead of yourself," he said slowly, repeating the words of his wife.

Sofia smiled through her tears. "Exactly."

Against his will, Theo pictured Emmie, imagining her holding their child tenderly, singing a low lullaby. He could see her beautiful, luminous face.

What did their baby look like now, at two months?

Would he suddenly be thirty, and a man—turning into an adult, as Sofia had suddenly, when Theo wasn't paying attention?

Had Emmie moved on, too, since he'd left? Had she given up on Theo and found a better man? Had she found a replacement father for their son?

Theo suddenly felt like he was on fire. He yanked off his tailored jacket, dropping it to the floor. Dripping with sweat, he unbuttoned the collar of his shirt.

"Emmie doesn't want me," he whispered. "I'm not good enough for her. Or our baby."

"If she thought that, why would she name the baby after you?"

He froze. "What?"

Digging into her purse, Sofia produced an invitation. "See?"

He snatched it up. Decorated with baby animals, the invitation listed the party details, along with the baby's weight, length, and name. *Theodore Karl Katrakis.* Emmie had named their child after him.

He knew his wife loved their baby more than her own life. Why would she name her adored son after the man who'd deserted them?

Was it possible she still loved him? Believed in him? In spite of everything he'd done to drive her away?

Love means putting the other person ahead of yourself.

Theo looked up with an intake of breath. His heart was racing like a motor as he turned to the divorce papers sitting beneath the cold sparkle of Emmie's diamond ring.

Was it too late?

Looking around his elegant cream-colored office with the oil paintings, he realized he'd been lying to himself about what he was doing in Paris.

All this time, he'd told himself he was pursuing his big dream, building a real-estate development blending mixed-use retail, housing and green space that would be his legacy.

The truth was the real thing he'd been building in Paris was a wall around his heart. Around *himself.*

The only way to be free was to let himself feel.

Forget being cold. Forget being strong.

The only way to live was to let himself love her.

Theo looked up with a gasp.

"I have to go," he told his sister, and grabbing the gift, he ran for the door.

* * *

The autumn evening was fresh and clear and cool. The sprawling terrace of the Ferraros' beachside mansion, with a view of the Atlantic, had been elaborately decorated for a baby shower, with colorful lights hanging across the trees with yellow and orange leaves, heaters between the tables to keep them warm.

Emmie had dressed up a bit for the occasion, beyond her usual T-shirt and jeans, wearing a soft pink dress that was comfortable and flattering to her still-curvaceous figure. Her hair was in a casual ponytail, but at least it was freshly washed. Her only makeup was tinted lip balm. She'd never win any beauty contests but she didn't need to. She didn't need to prove anything to anybody. She was Bear's mother, and Karl's daughter, and good with numbers, and a hard worker. She baked really good *fika* pastries, too, from her mother's recipes. Being on her own for the last two months, she'd had two choices: either collapse in despair or decide she was okay, just as she was. She had a baby to look after. So she'd decided to be okay.

"Thank you all for coming," Honora said as Nico left to put their yawning toddler Kara and baby Ivy to bed, and their household staff cleared the dinner plates from the tables. "Now—who's ready for some shower games?"

Honora was in her element as hostess. Now visibly pregnant, she'd welcomed them with her husband and young children, Honora's grandfather and his wife. Emmie's father was there, of course, and all four of her brothers, even Daniel, who'd flown all the way from Tulsa. Sam had also brought his girlfriend, Imani. Things were getting serious there.

Surrounded by her friends and family, Emmie had forced

herself to smile all night till her cheeks hurt, pretending she was enjoying herself. She wanted to.

She'd told Honora she wanted men allowed at her baby shower, which was traditionally a female affair, because she wanted her father and brothers there. Secretly, Emmie had hoped for a miracle. But by the time they'd mailed out the invitations last month, she'd realized how ridiculous her hope was, and she'd thrown Theo's invitation in the trash.

She needed to stop *hoping*. Longing for him, waiting for him, crying for him. Hope was poisoning her. She'd always love Theo. But he didn't love her. He didn't want to be married to her. He'd made that clear.

She had to let him go.

So two days ago, she'd filled out the divorce papers. She wondered how he'd reacted when he'd gotten them yesterday in Paris. She assumed he'd been relieved. She'd given him exactly what he wanted.

As October twilight fell across the ocean, Emmie surreptitiously wiped her eyes. She had to believe there was a better life waiting for her. She couldn't settle for unhappiness. She'd take inspiration from Harold Eklund, the elderly plumber she'd nearly married last June. She'd seen him in Queens last week, and he'd told her he was engaged to Luly Olsen, of the outrageous hats.

"I thought with my wife gone, I could never be happy again," he told Emmie. "I was going to settle for second best. But now, Luly and I…we're so in love. I guess it's never too late."

Emmie was glad for him. She didn't even mind being referred to as *second best* because for Harold, that's exactly what she'd been. Without love, what was the point?

Bear gurgled happily nearby from his bouncy seat, and

she focused back on her baby with a smile. But her throat still ached. Had she done the right thing?

"Are you happy, sweetheart?" her father asked quietly beside her. "Truly?"

She watched as her brothers bobbed for pacifiers—instead of apples—with the intense rivalry of a party game. Daniel rose from the bucket of water triumphantly with a pacifier in his teeth, his whole head wet.

Emmie smiled, though her heart was hurting. She took a deep breath. "Actually, Dad, I'm thinking of moving back to Queens."

"Really?" He looked astonished, then delighted. "What about the penthouse in Manhattan?"

"It's a little too fancy." She'd been lonely there since Theo left. High up in the sky, far from human contact, the huge triplex had felt isolating, imprisoning, not luxurious. "I'd rather get an apartment near you. Maybe I can set up to do bookkeeping, taxes and payroll for the neighborhood. I could work and still keep Bear with me."

"That sounds wonderful, honey. But…"

"But?"

Karl hesitated. "If you're moving to Queens, that must mean Theo, he…" He licked his lips. "The two of you, you're not…"

"No," she whispered, staring at her cup of punch. "We're not."

Her father took a deep breath, then reached for her hand. "I'm sorry, honey."

"Me, too." But Emmie did her best to smile, for the sake of the people she loved, who'd gone to so much trouble to celebrate her and Bear.

He was the best baby in the world, especially since he'd learned how to sleep five hours at a time at night. Always smiley—though, some uncharitable souls might declare it mere gas—he was growing plumper and more adorable by the day. She tried not to notice Theo's features in his face. Bear was his own person. And already the light of her life.

As they ate delicate little cakes and drank coffee, the wind grew cold off the Atlantic. In spite of the heat lamps, Emmie shivered in her dress and light cardigan in the autumn evening. If only things had been different. If only Theo could have been here, his handsome face smiling, his powerful arm over her shoulders.

Sitting on the cushioned furniture on the decorated terrace of the beach house, Emmie opened gifts for her baby, thanked her family and friends and didn't let herself cry.

"What's going on with Theo, Emmie?" Vince asked suddenly. Her eldest brother was sitting beneath a nearby heat lamp, holding her sleeping baby in his arms. He winced at their father's sharp glare, but persisted. "Why isn't he here?"

"Is your marriage over?" her brother Joe asked.

A lump rose in Emmie's throat. There was no point in hiding it from everyone. Even if it cast a pall over the evening, getting the truth out in the open would help her finally make a fresh start. Taking a deep breath, Emmie said slowly, "You might as well know... Theo and I—"

"Am I too late?"

Emmie's breath caught as she turned her head.

Theo stood in the doorway of the house, coming out onto the terrace. His tailored dark suit was wrinkled and rumpled, but somehow he'd never looked more handsome. The night breeze off the Atlantic ruffled his dark hair, as his black eyes met hers.

"Theo!" Honora hugged him, and Nico shook his hand.

But he had eyes only for Emmie. He came toward her

where she sat on the sofa beneath the round, colorful lights swaying in the dark trees.

Heart pounding, she looked up at him. "What are you doing here?"

"I brought you something." Pulling a small, beautifully wrapped present from his jacket pocket, he placed it in her hands. Trying to ignore the way she'd shivered at his touch—the night was cold—she unwrapped the package.

Inside, she found lumpy blue baby booties, clearly home-made. She looked up with an intake of breath.

"From Sofia," he explained.

Emmie told herself she'd treasure the gift from Bear's aunt, of course she would, but even so, she felt a swell of bitter disappointment. Licking her lips, she set the booties aside. "Thank you. It was kind of her." Then she frowned at him. "You flew here just to deliver it for her? All the way from Paris?" It seemed strange that Theo had agreed to such an errand.

"That wasn't the only reason," Theo said softly.

"Why…?" Suddenly she knew. "Oh. Of course. You came to New York to see your lawyer. About the divorce."

There was an intake of breath from friends and family at the word *divorce*. Theo didn't seem to notice or care. His dark eyes burned through her.

"Is there someone else, Emmie? Is that why you want it to end?"

Her jaw tightened as she said coldly, "I'm not the one who wanted it to end, Theo." Her gaze fell on Bear, snug-gled in her brother's arms on a nearby chair. "But yes. There's someone else."

Another gasp. Theo staggered back a step on the shad-owy terrace. As he rubbed his eyes, the plain gold band on his left hand gleamed in the lights.

"I… I really didn't think…" For a moment, he seemed unable to speak. Then he shook his head. "Good for you," he said hollowly. He forced a smile. "You deserve to be happy, Emmie. You deserve all the love in the world."

His handsome face was miserable. And suddenly, even after everything, it was hard for her to see him in pain.

Taking a deep breath, she straightened her spine. She didn't know what he was doing here, but she wasn't going to be his puppet, falling at his feet whenever he deigned to appear.

He'd made his choice. Now he could live with it.

"I know I do," she said coldly. "So does Bear."

"Bear?" he said guardedly.

Rising to her feet, Emmie collected their baby from her brother and brought him to her husband beneath the swaying lights. "It's our nickname for him."

"Bear." Theo exhaled, looking down at their baby in her arms, who was more adorable than ever in fuzzy footie pajamas. He cleared his throat, his expression oddly vulnerable as he said, "My sister's invitation said you named him after me."

Was that why Theo had come? To give her a hard time for their baby's name?

"Yes, well," Emmie glanced wryly at her father, who snorted and rolled his eyes, "*Theodore* is a lot of name for a baby. I started calling him Teddy. Then Dad called him Teddy Bear…"

"Then just Bear," Karl replied, smiling between his daughter and grandson, before glaring at his son-in-law.

"Bear. I like it." Theo looked at the baby. The infant now regarded his father with equal interest, and with the same black eyes. He said in wonder, "He's gotten so much bigger already."

"I know."

Theo licked his lips. She was staring at his mouth when she heard him say shyly, "Can I hold him?"

"Of course." Theo wanted to hold their baby? Trying to calm the pounding of her heart, telling herself this didn't mean anything, she helped him take the baby, showing him how to support his head.

As Theo held him, Emmie saw a swirl of emotion on her husband's handsome face she'd never seen before. Adoration. Fear. And something else. Something more…

"Thank you, Emmie." Theo looked up, and to her astonishment she saw a suspicious sheen in his eyes. "Even though our marriage is over, I'll always be grateful that you're his mother. The best woman in the world," he said softly. He swallowed. "I'll sign your divorce papers. But even if you love someone else now, I intend to be Bear's father. I'll always be there for him from now on." Looking at her with haunted yearning, he whispered, "And I'll always be here for you. For anything."

The look he gave her went far beyond desire. The floor suddenly trembled beneath Emmie's shoes. What was happening?

"It's Bear," she blurted out. "He's my someone else."

Theo blinked. His brow furrowed. "What?"

"The other man in my life now. It's Bear. Just Bear."

Her husband sucked in his breath, his wide black eyes searching hers. "Is it really true?"

Emmie lifted her chin. "But I still don't understand what you're doing here. Why you came all the way from Paris."

All her friends and family were staring between them in a breathless hush beneath the colorful lights leaving latticed shadows of the half-bare trees in the autumn night.

In the distance, she could hear the roar of the surf. Or was it the pounding of her heart?

Theo stepped forward, his dark eyes piercing her soul. "Is there a chance, Emmie?" he whispered. "Do I still have a chance?"

She trembled, caught by his gaze. Afraid to say a word. Afraid this was all a dream.

"Because if I thought I had a chance, I'd…"

"You'd what?" she said softly.

He took a shuddering breath. "I'd throw myself at your feet."

"Get the baby," her father muttered, and Nico discreetly plucked Bear out of Theo's arms.

Her husband turned to face her. And as he came forward, taking both her hands in his own, everyone and everything else around them vanished. She saw only him.

"Leaving you was the biggest mistake of my life," he said in a low voice. "For all my life, I've been scared to love anyone. The day we wed, I was terrified out of my mind."

Her jaw dropped. Theo Katrakis admitting fear? Aloud? In front of all her family and friends?

"Because I already knew what would happen," he continued. "I knew I'd fall in love with you. That I already had."

"What?" breathed Emmie. What had he said?

His hands tightened over hers. "What if I gave you my heart and you left? What if you died? What if I couldn't be the man you wanted? I didn't think I could survive it. So I tried my hardest to be like ice. To never let you in."

She was afraid to breathe. "And?"

His dark eyes flickered. Raising his hand, he stroked her cheek. "Your love melted my defenses," he whispered. "You left me bare. When you went into labor, I felt helpless.

Powerless. I felt panicked and ashamed. So I left you." His gaze fell on Bear, cuddled in Nico's arms. "Both of you."

Remembering that awful day, Emmie closed her eyes, feeling a painful twist in her heart. "You hurt me."

"I know. I'll never forgive myself. And I've been punished every day since. I ran away to be a big shot in Paris. To follow my so-called dream. And I learned something important."

"What?"

He took a deep breath. "The whole world is a wasteland without you. No matter how many palaces or gardens I build. Without the woman I love…this earth is as empty as my heart."

His voice cracked. He looked down at their intertwined hands. Then, as he'd threatened, he fell to his knees before her.

"Give me a chance to win you back, Emmie," he whispered, pressing her hand against his rough, unshaven cheek. "Tell me I have a chance to regain your trust. Whether it takes weeks or months. *Years.* All I ask is that you let me try." He looked up at her, and his eyes were luminous with tears. "Because I'm utterly, completely in love with you."

Emmie gasped. She heard her friends and family do the same.

"I love you, Emmie. And it's true what I said. You deserve a better man that me." He pressed his forehead to her clasped hands in a medieval, almost holy, gesture of fealty. "But if you give me the chance, I'll spend the rest of my life trying to be the man you deserve."

Beyond the terrace, beyond the shadows of autumn trees with their hanging lights, Emmie saw the sweep of moonlight over the black Atlantic waves. Could she forgive him? Could she let him back into her life—back into her heart?

A dozen people waited breathlessly for her answer. She closed her eyes, hearing the soft whir of the heat lamps, the call of seagulls in the cold October night.

Then she exhaled, opening her eyes. Reaching down, she pulled him to his feet. "I've always known you were a pain, Theo." Tears overflowed her lashes as she gave him a slow-rising smile. "And I've always known you're worth it."

He searched her gaze with an intake of breath. "Yes?"

"I never stopped hoping for a miracle. I never stopped loving you, Theo—"

"Oh, my darling," he whispered and pulled her into his arms. For a long moment, he just held her tight. Emmie closed her eyes, her cheek against his chest. She breathed in the scent of him, woodsy and masculine, and she felt like she'd finally come home.

"Kiss her!" someone yelled.

Lifting his head, Theo looked back with a grin at their friends and family. "I was thinking the same thing."

And he lowered his head to hers in a kiss of pure fire. Emmie dimly heard the wild roar of the surf, echoing the rush of blood in her veins, as his hot, sensual embrace told her everything she needed to know, pledging love forever… or maybe longer.

Their baby son, held too tightly by Nico, gave an indignant squawk. Theo and Emmie pulled apart with a laugh and reached to bring their son into their arms.

"I love you," Theo told his son, then he cupped Emmie's cheek. "And I love you, Emmie."

Around them, friends and family cheered, as if they had just turned from the altar, newly wed.

And that was how it felt to Emmie. Except instead of a bridal bouquet, Emmie held their baby. Instead of a glitzy diamond ring, she held her husband's powerful hand in her own. Instead of words vowing to love and cherish, she saw the promise in Theo's dark eyes.

And in that moment Emmie knew she'd be loved, seen and adored for the rest of her life. All her dreams, especially the ones she'd believed could never come true, were all around her.

EPILOGUE

IT WAS STRANGE, Theo reflected eight months later. For a man who'd once claimed to not want family, he now had quite a lot of it. Strange—and wonderful.

"Who gives this woman to be married to this man?"

Eyes stinging, Theo looked down at his sister in her white gown. "I do."

Placing Sofia's hand into her bridegroom's, Theo returned to sit with his wife in the front row of the white-washed Greek church.

Looking up with a tender smile, Emmie put her hand over his. Her emerald-cut diamond, now back in its rightful place on her left hand, glinted in the dim light. His heart swelled as he thought how much he loved her. He was the luckiest man on earth.

When the ceremony ended, Theo watched as the newly married couple kissed, then left the tiny church hand in hand. Fifty-odd guests followed them, walking the half mile to the new house that had been built in Lyra, over the ashes of Theo and Sofia's childhood home.

Well, not exactly. The new house had been built in a slightly different location, closer to the beach, their favorite place to play as children. On the spot where the old house had burned, where their mother had died, they'd built a garden, to remember and find peace, and they planted the roses their mother had once loved.

It was a lovely June morning. Walking with Emmie along the cliffside path, Theo breathed in the sea air. Emmie was wearing a soft, lovely dress, and he was dressed in a suit to match, pushing a top-of-the-line baby stroller.

At ten months, Bear was making happy *la-la-la* sounds, grabbing his own feet, his adorably chunky thighs sticking out of dapper blue shorts. The baby hadn't quite figured out how to walk yet, but the kid was so energetic, Theo fully expected once he learned he'd be running within the hour. There'd be no stopping him.

Just as there was no stopping his wife. Theo glanced at her as they walked. Even the beauty of Greece couldn't compare to Emmie's soulful, gorgeous voluptuousness. Her honey-blond hair tumbled over her shoulders, lit by the golden sun. Her violet eyes outshone both the vivid blue sky and sapphire-hued Aegean.

At four months pregnant, her belly was barely starting to show beneath her dress, but her breasts were already in full bloom. His gaze lingered on her breasts, then her exquisite pink lips. After a year of marriage, he still couldn't get enough of her body, her beauty and, most of all, her soul. Emmie was the heart of their family, which meant for Theo she was the heart of the world.

Emmie's extended family, her brothers, her brand-new sister-in-law, her father and even her father's new girlfriend were straggling behind them on the cliffside path, laughing and teasing each other. Theo had had to get a bigger private jet to bring them all here. He smiled. His jet was now their minivan.

But he found he liked the happy chaos of Emmie with

her four brothers. Five children sounded about right. He hoped this second baby would be just the start.

Ahead of them, Honora and Nico were walking with four-year-old Kara in her flower-girl dress, pushing their toddler Ivy and baby Jack in a double stroller. The Ferraros were now their neighbors. Theo and Emmie had sold the penthouse and bought a brick town house in Greenwich Village on their friends' small street. Their new house had seven bedrooms, a rooftop terrace and even—most luxurious of all in Manhattan—an actual backyard. Emmie was already hinting about getting a dog. As if there wasn't enough mayhem already, he thought ruefully. But now he knew there was always room for more. There was always more to love.

Though Theo occasionally still traveled for work, unless there was serious reason, he was always home every night at six. He often visited Paris to check progress but allowed his extremely competent employees to oversee the day-to-day project. That way, Theo was able to have dinner with his wife and son, read Bear bedtime stories, and give Emmie a break, a little shoulder rub and ask about her day before they fell passionately into bed.

He enjoyed his business. He *loved* his family.

Theo's life had changed so much. He no longer tried to be cold to avoid hurt or the possibility of loss. Those were just part of the package with feeling love and joy. They all went together.

So he embraced it. All of it. It was the bravest thing he'd ever done. And the hardest. And the best.

Control was an illusion. Love was real.

Dancing with his wife at his little sister's wedding reception, held in a big white tent beside the Aegean, Theo laughed with delight as they swayed ineptly to the loud, raucous music of the French rock band his sister and her new husband adored. Surrounded by the newlyweds' young, cheering friends and the even noisier cheering of Theo's big new family, he felt his heart was a million miles wide.

"Are you crying?" Emmie whispered.

He rubbed his eye. "Got some dirt in my eyes."

By her knowing smile, she wasn't fooled, which was fine, because he didn't intend her to be. Theo wanted his wife to know him, both the good and bad, and for him to have the gift of knowing the good and bad of her. Though, as he teased her, he had yet to find any bad. But when it came, he would accept it with open arms, as she'd accepted him.

Emmie had given him a second chance, when he hadn't really deserved a first one. He would love her till the end of his days.

Nuzzling her neck on the dance floor, he whispered, "You're the most beautiful woman here. Anywhere."

"Oh, stop."

Theo looked down at her tenderly. "I mean it."

She blushed, looking down, hiding a smile. "You have to say that because I'm your wife."

"I have to say it," he said and stroked wonderingly through her long blond hair, "because it's true."

And as he lowered his head to kiss her, right there on the dance floor, surrounded by people they loved in the big reception tent, Theo knew Emmie had given him more than family. She'd given him his life.

* * * * *